Requiem for the Status Quo

Irene Frances Olson

BLACK ROSE
writing™

ISBN: 978-1-61296-898-8
PUBLISHED BY BLACK ROSE WRITING
www.blackrosewriting.com

Printed in the United States of America
Suggested Retail Price (SRP) $18.95

Requiem for the Status Quo is printed in Palatino Linotype

Dedicated to my father, Don Patrick Desonier, who wore his disease with the dignity it did not deserve. I love you, Dad.

ACKNOWLEDGEMENTS

From the very first day I decided to become a novelist, my husband, Jerry, supported me on my quest. If it weren't for him – for so very many reasons – this book would have never made it into the hands of readers. My Beta readers, starting with my daughter, Erin Green, who believed in the story as much as I did. Her no-holds-barred input was much appreciated. A few of my other Beta readers: brother, Don Desonier; sister, Mary Riesche; Dr. Emory Hill, PhD, who encouraged me not to sugarcoat the disease; Polly Miller, long-term care industry professional, one of my greatest fans, who read every page of every version of my novel and who cried each and every time; Anne Leigh Parrish, published author of short stories and novels, and the best cheerleader a writer could have; Pacific Northwest Writers Association (PNWA) who provided vital professional input; and finally, to my mother, Patricia Desonier, who let me pretend to be a writer way back when I was five years old and shamelessly applauded my elementary efforts.

Praise for
Requiem for the Status Quo

"In this stunning debut novel, Irene Frances Olson depicts with tenderness and grace one family's struggle to cope with the devastation of Alzheimer's disease."
– **Anne Leigh Parrish**, author of *Women Within*

"As someone who has spent her career in the senior housing industry, I deem *Requiem For The Status Quo* a winner on two levels: It is an endearing story of the love between a daughter and a father, and it provides the reader with practical insight into the challenges faced by our aging population."
– **Polly Miller**, former Chief Marketing Officer, *AegisLiving*

"A heartfelt and compelling story, relevant to so many family households across the globe, REQUIEM is a must-read for all generations."
– **Dwayne Clark**, Chairman & CEO of TRUE Productions, a film production company created from the love of storytelling

"Ms. Olson's experience as a long-term care ombudsman, coupled with her own Alzheimer's caregiving experience, make her more than qualified to tell the story of families in turmoil, thrust into the learn-as-you-go task of caregiving."
– **Vicki Elting**, Assistant Washington State LTC Ombudsman

Requiem for the
Status Quo

ONE

Patrick couldn't understand why everyone was honking their horn at him. Sure, he was driving a wee bit under the posted speed limit, but he was in the far right lane of one of the busiest sections of the I-5 freeway just north of Seattle where slower drivers were supposed to be. He simply wanted to be sure not to miss his exit off the freeway so he was paying extra attention. He and his daughter, Colleen, had a date that afternoon to watch a baseball game on television; he wanted to be certain to get home on time for the first pitch.

Truth be told, Patrick was mighty worried because it had never taken him this long to get home from the South Seattle Home Depot. He'd feel a lot better about the protracted trip if he had found the crocosmia bulbs he wanted for the front walkway; instead, he's headed home without anything to show for his efforts.

When a driver in one of those over-sized pickup trucks sped up close behind him flashing his high beams and honking his horn, Patrick glanced at his dashboard and was surprised to see the needle barely registering 35 on the speedometer. Fearing there must be something mechanically wrong with his old Caddy, he decided to pull over onto the cement shoulder, barely avoiding being rear-ended. As he did so, the young man who had been right behind him gave Patrick the one-finger salute that many drivers are so fond of giving. Once safely on the shoulder, Patrick turned off the ignition, retrieved the vehicle manual from the glove box, and looked through the Troubleshooting section.

Sometime later there was a knock on the Caddy's passenger window. "Sir? Is there something I can help you with?"

Patrick was startled when he saw the rather imposing law enforcement officer looking at him through the window. Patrick rolled down the window and said, "Oh, uh, good afternoon Officer, uh, I'm just fine, thank you, how are you?"

"It's really not safe for you to be parked on the side of the freeway. May I see your driver's license and car registration please?"

Patrick hunted through his already open glove box, all the while trying to come up with a decent reason for his choice of parking space on the freeway. "You know, Officer—I think you'll find this to be rather amusing—for some reason or another I got discombobulated and can't quite find the right exit to get back home." Patrick leaned toward the passenger window, holding his documents out to the officer. "Here you go, sir, my driver's license and registration. You'll see that my license is current and so are my car tabs."

"I see that . . . Mr. Quinn. How about I give you a ride home?" The State Trooper tilted his large wide-brimmed hat back on his neck a bit, examined the inside of the Eldorado and didn't see anything amiss, except for the look of confusion on the elderly man's face.

"That's very kind of you, Officer, but I don't want my neighbors to have something to talk about even more than they already do with me stepping out of your squad car and all. Can you just tell me how far away I am from the exit to my Wallingford neighborhood? I live on Sunnyside Avenue North, not far from St. Benedict's Catholic Church."

The State Trooper pulled off his hat, scratched his head, looked south, then back at Patrick, and scratched his head again. "Sir, I'm afraid you drove too far north. You over-shot your exit by at least eight miles."

"You don't say?"

"As I see it, you're going to need to drive another half mile north and get off the freeway at 175th. Once you drive over the 175th overpass, you'll see the entrance for I-5 South on the left so on 175th, you'll want to get into the far left lane right away to make your turn."

Not at all clear on the driving instructions, nonetheless Patrick wanted this conversation with law enforcement to come to a close so he said, "Got it, I'm sure I'll be fine now Officer. Have a nice day!" Patrick gave the Trooper a thumbs up sign but the officer didn't budge.

"Mr. Quinn, I'd much rather drive you myself, but I tell you what, let's compromise. I'll drive a car-length ahead of you—keep in mind, the speed limit is sixty miles per hour so you'll need to quickly gather speed—and eventually get us going south towards Wallingford. Once I see that you've taken the 45th Street exit behind me I'll trust you to get back home in one piece. Is that a deal?"

Patrick wrinkled his nose, looked to his left at the fast moving traffic, then out the passenger window toward the officer. "I guess that's fair, lead the way!"

The officer told Patrick that he would turn on the squad car's lights in order to usher Patrick's car safely off the shoulder and into the flow of traffic. That was a concession that, although embarrassing, would be extremely helpful; there's no way he could have blended in with the fast-moving cars without expert law enforcement assistance. As soon as the Trooper edged off the shoulder with lights flashing and siren whoop-whooping, Patrick checked his left side mirror, the rearview mirror, the side mirror again, and then floored the Caddy to get caught up with the squad car.

· · · · ·

I arrived at my dad's Craftsman style house from my condo right around four-thirty, fully expecting him to be home because we had a date to watch the Seattle Mariners baseball game against the New York Yankees, but Dad's car wasn't in the driveway. "Huh, that's odd, there's no way he would miss that team matchup." Thankfully, I had a key to the house so I put the meatloaf in the oven and the other dinner makings into the fridge. To kill time and distract myself from worrying about him, I set up TV trays at our respective places in front of the television, set each tray with utensils and Mariners fan napkins, and waited.

Five minutes later I checked my cell phone to remind myself of when Dad had called to tell me he was going to Home Depot, wondering if my internal clock was all out of whack. Nope, he called at two o'clock and said he'd be at the house no later than three-thirty.

I decided to call my brother to find out if he knew anything of Dad's whereabouts. "Jonathan, hi, um, have you heard from Dad this afternoon?"

"Was I supposed to?"

I pulled aside the voile curtains and looked out the front window, hoping to see Dad's old battleship of a car pulling into the driveway. "Sorry, no, he wasn't necessarily supposed to call you, but I'm at his house now and he's not here. We're scheduled to watch the Mariners game at six so he should have been home long before this."

"Maybe he ran to the grocery store, I'm sure he'll be home soon. Listen, Colleen, I've gotta go. Melanie, Kirby and I are actually attending that game and if we don't leave now we'll never find decent parking."

"Okay, I was just worried, is all, but you know, he told me he was going to the Home Depot and then right home, that was almost three hours ago."

"Home Depot on a Saturday is a zoo, I'm sure he's just held up because of the crowds. Text me if he's not home by five, but sis, I've gotta go."

"Okay . . . but Jonathan?" Colleen at long last saw her dad pull into the driveway. "Never mind, he just got home, enjoy the game." Colleen abruptly hung up and slipped her phone in her back pocket.

"Colleen, I'm home!"

Huh, Dad wanted to pretend nothing was wrong, I decided to go with it until my curiosity could get the best of me. "I brought over a batch of your favorite meatloaf and put it in the oven to re-heat. Other than boiling the potatoes for mashing and serving up the salad, looks like we'll have a pretty easy dinner. Does the menu sound okay with you?"

He said it all sounded great and immediately disappeared into the bathroom. When he joined me in the kitchen he said, "Nice weather we're having, eh, sweetie?"

Not wanting to baby my eighty-four-year-old father, I tried not to get on him for his unexplained lengthy absence, thinking, *what could go wrong on a Wallingford to Home Depot outing? Maybe it's nothing at all, I'm probably overreacting. Forget that, who am I kidding?*

"So Dad, you said you'd be home way before I arrived but when I got here you were nowhere to be found. Did you have car trouble or something?"

"Why are you giving me such a hard time, Colleen? So I was a little late, maybe I met up with my Korean War pals for a cup of coffee, or maybe I took the long way home. There's no need for you to read me the riot act."

Whoa, that didn't sound like the cool, calm, and collected dad that never raised his voice. I walked over to him, gave him a hug, and held him at arm's distance. "What's got into you? All I said was that I was concerned that your trip seemed to take longer than expected. I think I have a right to worry when you weren't here when you said you'd be."

Oh, oh, Dad had tears in his eyes—I didn't expect that. I led him to his chair at the dining table. "Why don't we sit down and have a cup of tea and talk about it, okay? Come on, take a load off." While I put the water on to boil and set out the mugs and teabags, I gave him time to compose himself.

When I joined him at the table, he reached across the dinette table and took both my hands in his. "Sweetie, I'm so ashamed. I got lost coming home from the store and ended up parked on I-5 trying to get my bearings."

"Oh Dad, I'm so sorry."

"And to make matters worse, a State Trooper pulled over to check on me, and when I told him I was lost, he offered to drive me home. I couldn't let him do that, it would have been embarrassing for me and I didn't want the neighbors to think I'd gotten into some kind of trouble with the law."

I refrained from giggling at the thought that Dad could ever get into that kind of mischief and instead I delved further into his driving dilemma. "So tell me, is this the first time you've been confused while driving?"

Oh, oh, more tears.

"Dad?"

"Truthfully?"

"I think that would be advisable."

"It's happened a few times before but never on the freeway. When it's happened in the past, I've been able to pull over to a safe place, collect my thoughts, and get to where I needed to be. But this time, I'm telling you, I was so mixed up, I just about got out of my vehicle to walk home."

Mercy, that's a sight I didn't ever want to see. "You were smart to stay in your car. Freeways aren't meant for casual strolls, you could have gotten killed." I squeezed his fingers. "Please promise you'll never get out of your car if you get stuck on the freeway again." I stood up, prepared our tea, gave Dad his mug, and rejoined him at the table.

Dad dipped his teabag up-down, up-down, up-down, to the point where I thought he had forgotten I was sitting right across from him. "Dad?"

He placed his teabag on the Formica table, blew over the top of his mug, took a sip, and then looked me in the eye. "I wonder if perhaps it might be a good time for me to stop driving, you know, sell the car. I bet I could get good money for a classic Caddy like mine."

My poor dad was suggesting something that most people, especially men, would find hard to do: give up the car keys and rely on others for transportation. Now the tears started to pool in my eyes. I wiped a tear that inched down my cheek, stood up, and stepped behind my dad. I placed my arms around his shoulders and neck, and kissed him on the scantily clad top of his head. "I think that's a fabulous idea, how about we ask Jonathan to take charge of making all the necessary arrangements? Being the salesman that he is, I think he could sweet talk just about anyone into just about any vehicle and get top dollar."

Dad shook his head; maybe he was having second thoughts. I moved to his right and got eye level with him. "I promise, between me and that brother of mine, you'll always have transportation to wherever you need to go."

He took another sip of his tea.

"What do you say, shall we give Jonathan a call about selling your car?"

Dad turned to me. "What a terrific idea, I wish I'd thought of that."

"Okay, we'll do that real soon, but right now, let's get our dinner ready so we can watch the Mariners beat those damn Yankees."

"Oh, that's right, there's a Mariner game tonight, why don't we watch the game?"

"Gee, why didn't I think of that?"

TWO

When Dad and I arrived at our car in the St. Benedict Church parking lot, I was finally able to release the laughter I had tamped down through the second half of Mass. "Can you believe that guy in front of us snoring through the entire sermon? If ever there was a contest for *Loudest Snoring During A Boring Sermon* that guy would take first place."

Dad doubled over with laughter and placed a hand on the top of the Subaru's roof. "I almost poked him in the back to get him to stop, but his snoring was the highlight of Father Bill's sermon."

I helped Dad into the passenger seat. "I agree, Father Bill was really off his game today. I was more interested in trying to guess how long it would take for the guy's wife to smack him upside the head. The looks she gave him were priceless."

I must have said something awfully funny because now Dad's whooping like a hyena while struggling to buckle his seat belt. "Your mother did that to me once."

I got in the car, turned to Dad, and caught the mischievous look on his face. "No way, were you in church at the time?"

He slapped his knee, "Darn right. The worst part was that it happened during a church member's eulogy. The guy who died had been a member of the Knights of Columbus for a long, long time so the Supreme Knight came from the East Coast to deliver the eulogy. I guess because of the distance he traveled, the guy thought he had to get his money's worth. By the time I fell asleep, he had been droning on for about half an hour."

I backed the car out of the parking space and headed out of the church parking lot. "Did Mom actually hit you on the head or did she just elbow you? I can't see her hitting you."

"Oh, she elbowed me at first but that didn't do the trick. That's when she hit me on the head." Dad broke out in another round of laughter.

"There must be more to the story for you to be splitting a gut just telling it."

"Her hit startled me so much, I figured there must be some sort of response I missed out on so I shouted, 'Amen!' as loud as can be."

"You didn't!"

"I'm afraid I did. Your mother wouldn't have anything to do with me after that. She tapped the lady to her right and asked to trade places with her, but the gal would have none of that, your mother was stuck with me. But I have to say, I had the last laugh because the Supreme Knight took my outburst as a hint to end the eulogy. During the coffee time afterwards a few of the male church members came up to me and thanked me for putting an end to the guy's jabbering."

"So you were a hero then?"

"Well, to some, but not your mother, at least not right away."

"Oh? Do tell."

"She kept to herself most of the day but then I heard her laughing in the kitchen. She was stirring the soup pot and saying, 'Amen! Amen!' and shaking her head. When I joined her in the kitchen, she looked at me with tears rolling down her cheek and said, 'You sure put that guy in his place. Amen!'"

That cracked me up. "I didn't figure Mom would stay mad very long." For the rest of the drive, I considered that if anyone were to witness some our conversations we would be considered uncouth—but they would be wrong. Most of the Quinn family members found amusement in even the most mundane situations. With the exception of my brother, we tried not to take ourselves too seriously.

Dad sat up straight in his seat and folded his hands in his lap. "I guess now that we're getting close to the cemetery, we should become very somber when we visit your mother." Another quick look at him and I matched his serious tone. "For sure, she'd turn over in her grave hearing us talk this way."

Then we both cracked up knowing that the opposite would be true. Mom married a jokester because she was a jokester herself.

$$\bullet \quad \bullet \quad \bullet \quad \bullet \quad \bullet$$

I parked the car near a beautiful section of Calvary Cemetery heavily populated with pink-flowered cherry trees. This is the section where Mom was buried two years ago after dying suddenly from a heart attack caused by an arterial embolism. She had felt kind of "out of it" a few days prior but none of the family expected those somewhat innocuous feelings would lead to her death. Dad managed to put it all in perspective for us as we reeled from our sudden loss. Apparently Mom had mentioned several times over the years that when her time came, she wanted to die in her sleep. I guess God must have been listening, because that's exactly what happened.

With very few exceptions, Dad and I visit Mom after Mass every Sunday. Although I used to be a twice-a-year Catholic, I've benefited from this comforting ritual as much as Dad has. As a widow myself with an embarrassingly stunted social life, going to Mass and visiting Mom give me something worthwhile to do on Sunday.

Dad headed on his own to the right-hand side of the cemetery and signaled for me to join him. "Hop to it slow-poke, let's go see your mother."

"Hey Dad, why are you heading over there? Mom's over on this side."

He looked to the right, then back at me. "I think I know where your mother is laid to rest, come on, time's a-wastin'."

When this type of temporary memory lapse occurs, I'm always torn between insisting and complying, but I invariably choose the route that gives Dad the benefit of the doubt. After I caught up with him, I linked my arm through his and let him lead me to where he believed Mom was buried.

I took a deep breath. "Can you smell the cherry blossoms? It's a lot stronger than last week."

"Is that what I'm smelling? It's kind of like a musty rose smell, I like it, and I'm happy your mother is surrounded by her favorite color."

After a few more steps Dad stopped at a salmon-colored headstone. "Here she is, just where I told you she'd be." He looked closely at the lettering on the stone, removed his glasses, cleaned them with his handkerchief, and took a second look. "That's strange, who's this Carl Shepherd guy and what has he done with my Connie?"

I took Dad's hand and made light of the situation. "You know what? I understand why you thought Mom's resting place was in this area, her headstone was placed under a cherry tree just like this one." I pointed to the left, "But I think it might be more towards that way, wanna give it a try?"

"I'm sure you're right, but how could I forget where my bride of forty-eight years is buried?" Then slapping his forehead he added, "Oh my God, I've misplaced your mother! Don't tell your brother. Jonathan would have a cow." Shaking his head, he said, "That kid has no sense of humor."

"Ain't that the truth? Now let's get going, we don't want to keep Mom waiting."

"Yeah, she may give up on us and high-tail it out of here."

And yet again I was glad no one else was privy to our banter.

. . . . .

After our late lunch at Blue Star Café, I headed home knowing Dad would spend the balance of the afternoon in his Wallingford bungalow reading the Sunday paper and watching the local and national news programs. Back at my Queen Anne-area condo, Ramona, my Border collie, was good and ready for a walk, so after I changed my clothes we walked to the off-leash area of Kinnear Park for a round of catch. This is our favorite park: Ramona gets to exercise and I get to feast my eyes on the unparalleled panoramic view of downtown Seattle from the top of Queen Anne with its varying heights of architecturally challenged buildings, Elliott Bay with its competing boat and seaplane traffic, and the Space Needle—an observation tower that is one of the few structures left over from the 1962 World's Fair.

After a dozen or so fetch and releases Ramona lost interest in the saliva-laden tennis ball, and deserted me to join up with the other canines to do what canines do: sniff, greet, and play their doggie games.

I plopped onto one of the benches and pulled out my phone in the hopes that my older sister, Patty, had time for a daddy update. "Hey beautiful, how are you on this early spring day?"

"Hey yourself, I'm doing fine but I bet your weather is more comfortable than ours. We're at 95 degrees right now."

I don't know how my sister tolerates that arid California weather. "Ugh, you can have it. It doesn't need to be any warmer than seventy for me to feel like I'm getting a good weather day in Seattle. You should have seen the cherry blossoms at Calvary today, pink blossoms everywhere."

"So how is Dad doing, did you guys have a good visit with Mom?"

I let out my breath. "It was fine, but Dad had another senior moment, one you won't believe."

"What, did he forget it was Sunday?"

"No, nothing like that, but he forgot where Mom's buried. You know the parking lot near Mom's section?

"It's been awhile, but I think so."

"Instead of walking to the left like we'd done more than a hundred times, he insisted Mom was buried to the right. So I humored him and walked to where he was certain she was laid to rest, but, of course, another person was buried there instead."

"Oops."

"I know, in true Dad style, he made light of it and even joked that he'd misplaced Mom."

"That's our dad all right."

"We both had a chuckle over it but the whole episode was pretty eye-opening for me, and even though he turned the moment into a funny interlude, I'm pretty sure it bothered him."

"Hey, Colleen?"

"Yeah?"

"I think the doctor's diagnosis of senior moments may have underestimated Dad's problem a bit. From what you've told me the past couple months, it sounds like he has a dementia kind of thing, not just a brain fart."

"Yeah, for sure not just a brain fart, him forgetting Mom's headstone location was pretty telling."

"I have to agree with you. So what's next?"

"I know I need to do a better job of tracking the severity of the episodes, you know, being more diligent about writing them down in my *Dad Journal*, and I should review it more often. If I do that I can more effectively compare recent brain glitches with previous ones to figure out if what Dad says and does is normal, or whether he's experiencing a new normal."

"Isn't normal just normal?"

I do so much internet research on our dad's memory issues, I often forget that not everyone I come in contact with has read up on this stuff as much as me. "New normal is a phrase I see mentioned in lots of the research I've done. Pretty much it means that what used to be normal becomes a thing of the past when it's replaced by a new normal. That happens a lot—not just for those with cognitive decline, but anyone who's on an open-ended disease journey."

"Dang, you sound like one super intelligent human being."

With a false attitude of offense, I said, "Contrary to public opinion, I'm not as dumb as I look."

"Thank goodness for that."

I laid my head on the back of the bench and smiled, glad that my sister's sense of humor was alive and well and flowing through our cell phone lines. Drawing out my response, I said, "A-n-y-w-a-y, bottom line is that I'm going to pay more attention to the nuances in Dad's symptoms so we'll have a better sense of what's what."

"Good idea, and if I notice anything *new normal-ly* when I talk to Dad on the phone, I'll let you know. Deal?"

"Deal."

Ramona ran up to me, obviously exhausted from her playtime. "Ramona just told me she wants to go home and have dinner so I'd better get going."

"Okay, but hold on a sec. If I haven't said so recently, thanks for all the stuff you do for Dad. He's lucky to have you, and so are Jonathan and I." Patty huffed out a sigh. "Does Jonathan help out at all? I mean crap, he and Melanie live in Ballard. If I remember correctly, that's less than five miles from Wallingford."

"Yeah, yeah, but if Jonathan was more involved, he'd have more opportunities to make Dad feel ashamed about his memory lapses and I'm not gonna let that happen. I'd rather keep things as they are."

"I suppose you're right. I love you Colleen, thanks for

everything."

"No problem. I hope you know I'm happy to be the point person where Dad is concerned." I looked around the park to gather my thoughts, spotting a couple young families having picnics.

"Still there?"

"Yeah, I'm here. I was just thinking about the similarities in our situations—Dad's and mine, I mean. A few weeks after Mom died, Dad told me he understood what it felt like for me to lose Allan and suddenly be single when that's the last thing I ever expected to be. Up until he said that I hadn't looked at our dad as being a single man— but of course he is—and quite frankly, I hadn't thought of myself as single either. Since my marriage ended because of Allan's car accident—not because our relationship ended—for a few years after I still felt married to him, so the loss seemed far more acute. Dad feels the same way about Mom, and take it from someone who knows, it's a lousy feeling."

"Oh, Colleen, I'm so sorry."

"It's okay . . . I'm okay, I just wanted you to know that my connection with Dad—first as a result of Mom's death and then because of Dad's aging issues—is something I enjoy and nothing you need to worry about. Dad and I are fine."

"Me worry? Nah. Now you'd better get Ramona home and make sure you give her lots of my love."

"Will do. Talk to you later."

I reattached Ramona's leash, gave her some of my sister's love vibes, and headed home for a relaxing Sunday evening to try out a new Food Network recipe.

THREE

It had been two months since Dad misplaced Mom at the cemetery; fortunately he didn't repeat that mistake during subsequent visits. I guess that's good, but what I think really happened is that he surrendered control of that activity to me, not wanting to be found guilty of losing Mom again. I tried, and failed, to wear the same armor of denial worn by my brother, Jonathan, for the past year and a half but I just wasn't comfortable doing so. I continued to worry about how serious Dad's memory issues might be, but I took comfort in the plan I'd made with Patty to look out for any significant cognitive changes and more accurately document those changes for comparison's sake. Just the fact that I was moving forward, rather than stagnating in disbelief like my brother seemed to be doing, made me feel like I was doing something positive for Dad.

With wedding season in full swing I was super busy at *Brides by Sarah*, the bridal salon where I have worked for the past five years. With full appointment schedules on Saturdays, we often ignored callers and let them go to voicemail. Our first priority? The clients who were in the store from the start of the work day at ten in the morning, to the close of the salon doors at six.

About three hours into another work day—when I had just finished taking dress measurements of a mother of the bride—one of the sales associates, Cassandra, took me aside to say that my dad had left three voicemails for me. While I wrote the MOB's measurements onto a store order form, I tried to get a sense from Cassandra for how my dad sounded on the phone.

"So, did my father sound okay?"

"First of all, I'm sorry for listening to your father's messages but I was trying to get us caught up with incoming calls so we could make call-backs. In answer to your question, I'm not sure if he is okay. Like, in the first voicemail, all he said was for you to call him. About a half hour later he called to ask you where you put the laundry detergent."

"Sounds pretty harmless so far." Then I looked at her. "Was it?"

Cassandra bit her lip, looked down at the message pad, and then up at me, as if she was afraid to give me the third message.

"Just tell me what he said, I'm sure it's not as bad as you think."

"I think it is, Colleen. Your dad said he found the bottle of blue liquid soap underneath the kitchen sink—"

"No."

Cassandra delivered the remainder of the message at top speed. "And then he said that a cup of detergent must have been too much because lots of bubbles were flowing out of the washing machine and then he hung up."

I cupped my hand over my mouth, closed my eyes, and quickly opened them because I didn't like what I imagined—a wave of dish soap bubbles pouring out of the clothes washer lid. "Oh boy, that doesn't sound good at all."

"I'm sorry, but I thought you'd want to know."

"Oh, I wanted to know, um, what time did that last message come in?"

Cassandra looked at the message pad and cringed. "12:11. Yikes, that's almost two hours ago."

I handed the dress order form to Cassandra and asked her to finish up with the customer by getting the client's dress deposit, providing her with an estimate of when the dress would be ready for pick up, and gifting the client with one of our "Thank you for your order" Starbucks gift cards. With that taken care of, I chanced a call to my brother to see if he could resolve the bubble disaster at Dad's house.

"Oh, hi Melanie, sorry to disturb you on Saturday but I called Jonathan's cell and it went to voicemail. I really need to talk to him, is he around?"

"You're not disturbing me, but I'm afraid your brother is at Sahalee for a round of golf. Can I help with anything?"

I explained the situation and angel that she is, Melanie agreed to head over to Dad's house with my teenage nephew in tow; apparently Kirby was just sitting around moping because he was grounded for a curfew violation. I hoped that between the two of them, they could mitigate the damages and any panic Dad might be experiencing.

It was time to call him. "Hi Dad, are you floating out the front door yet?"

"Hi sweetie, not floating but definitely ankle-deep in suds. We must have bought the wrong detergent because it's never acted this way before. On the brighter side, at least the carpet won't need to be shampooed any time soon."

Some bright side, I mused. "I'm sorry it took me so long to call you back. We were swamped at the store and by the time one of us could check voicemail it was too late, but Melanie and Kirby are on their way to give you a hand. Kirby appears to have an open schedule today so he should be a big help."

"My goodness, I haven't seen that fella in quite some time. I was just telling your mother the other day how much I missed seeing our grandson. How old is he now?"

Dad's talking to Mom now? When did that start? And I couldn't believe we were having this conversation while he was slogging around in a bubble-sodden house and my staff was trying to juggle clients without the added benefit of their senior sales person. "Kirby's sixteen, and Dad, I need to get back to work. I'll come over once I'm done at the salon and we'll heat up leftovers for dinner, sound good?"

"I thought you were at work. You getting your hair done?"

"No, sorry, sometimes people call a bridal store a salon, but that's not important. Do my dinner plans sound okay?"

"Sure, that'll be hunky dory. What day is it today?"

Oh my gosh I love my dad but I have to get off the phone. "It's Saturday, but Dad—"

"I figured it was either Saturday or Sunday. If it's Saturday—"

"It is . . ." I turned my hand in front of me in a quick circle in an effort to make him speak faster.

"Since it's Saturday, I get to watch a baseball game on television, that'll keep me busy until you get here."

"Okay, I better go now, the store is filled with a passel of brides that need some tender loving care, but I'll see you later. Love you."

• • • • •

The afternoon flew by and thanks to Sarah's ongoing generosity and understanding, I left the store an hour early, picked Ramona up from my place to accompany me to Dad's, and had a relaxed, yet somewhat soggy, evening. And speaking of generosity, Melanie promised to make her husband—my brother—hire and pay for a professional to further remediate the water-damaged area of the house. Turns out Dad's floor was in need of a professional's touch. Fortunately, he had the wherewithal to turn off the washer as soon as he noticed the bubble waterfall, thus limiting the water damage to the laundry room and a few feet into the carpeted dining room, but those few feet of soggy carpet did a number on the wood subfloor.

During dinner I questioned Dad about his earlier comment about talking to Mom. Turns out he takes comfort in conversing with her spirit, but I assume it's a one-way conversation. Anyway, I remembered doing the same after Allan died so I concluded that Dad's practice of talking to my mom was normal, not something related to his brain that I needed to worry about.

I slept well that night feeling slightly better now that one more person was added to the caregiving team comprised of myself, my sister Patty, and my best friend, Pilar. Turns out, my sister-in-law had no idea of how much help Dad needed and was shocked at how much of that need was met by me. Now that she was clued in, she committed to helping out in any way she could which made me feel pretty darn good. Being stuck at work and not immediately able to meet Dad's need forced me to realize that I probably couldn't do it all. I still wanted to do it all, but this time I had to rely on someone else. Just knowing it was okay to delegate a task to another person took some of the pressure off me.

FOUR

For several months I diligently documented Dad's memory lapses—previously known as the more inane "senior moments"—as well as those Patty relayed to me from her phone conversations. I'm now on my second *Dad Journal* filled with red sticky notes on pages that reflect incidents that seem more troubling than others. I'm never without that journal; it goes with me to work at the bridal salon, on outings with Dad, and it's with me today as Ramona and I ride the 11:21 a.m. ferry to Whidbey Island for an overnight stay at Pilar Madrigal's house.

What a gem of a friend she has been through my current challenges, and way before that when I lost my husband of ten years in a fatal car accident. On a sunny day six-plus years ago, Allan left his job in Tukwila having just called to say he was on his way home. That was the last time we ever spoke. Five blocks from our house, a drunk driver ran a red light and my sweetheart was broadsided on the driver's side and killed instantly. Becoming a widow at forty-three years of age knocked the wind out of me; it did a darn good job of shaking my faith as well. I'm so grateful for my buddy Pilar; I couldn't hazard a guess as to how I'd be if her friendship hadn't been the soft place where I landed time and time again, and where I was about to land this weekend.

As the ferry from Mukilteo inched closer to the Clinton dock on the south side of Whidbey, Ramona strained at the leash wanting to chase the seagulls that mercilessly taunted her while I leaned over the railing in an attempt to force the boat to go faster. It had been three months since my best friend and I had seen each other, but we talked on the phone fairly frequently. Earlier this week Pilar sensed that my concern over Dad had ratcheted up several notches, so she didn't take "no" for an answer when she suggested I take a couple days off to head north for a visit. How do people get by without a little, or a lot, of help from a friend? Thankfully, I've never had to find out.

Standing at the Clinton side of the passenger exit, my hippy-wannabe friend stood ready to greet us in her predictable fashion—with arms opened wide.

"There're my girls, welcome back to my island."

Pilar and I hugged the living daylights out of each other while Ramona and Pilar's Chesapeake Bay retriever, Tristan, reacquainted themselves and then scampered over to the dog relief area out of respect for Ramona's full bladder.

Pilar took a step back and furrowed her eyebrows. "What's happened to the rest of ya'? You're skin and bones!"

"Don't be so dramatic. I lost a few pounds but I'm hardly a skeleton. But look at you, those jogging pointers I gave you the last time I was here sure paid off. You look a lot more buff than before." I turned Pilar around 180 degrees and added, "And you're starting to get a nice butt."

"You got it sista, next time you see me you won't recognize me."

We both cracked up at that not-quite-true statement and while I carried Ramona's backpack, Pilar took charge of my roll-on case as we reclaimed the dogs and loaded ourselves into Pilar's Volkswagen Bug—quite a feat for two adult humans and two dogs.

Pilar's island home is what most people might imagine a Pacific Northwest house would look like: an outside that resembles a log cabin but is a bit more modern than that, tongue and groove knotty pine walls inside—except for the water side of the house that sports floor to ceiling windows—a comfortably furnished living room whose focal point is the large wood-burning brick fireplace, and a galley type kitchen with lots of pine cabinets and retro enamel-faced appliances that look like they're right out of the 1950s, but aren't. The pièce de résistance, however, is the wrap around deck that faces Holmes Harbor and provides a front row seat to some of the most beautiful sunsets the Washington Coast has to offer.

I put my travel case in the Colleen Strand Guest Room at the top of the stairs and took in the view of the bay with Tristan and Ramona being teased by the lapping water created by passing boats. I asked myself how just a half hour after arriving on Whidbey Island, the stress of the past few months could be so thoroughly replaced by a serenity that enveloped me from head to toe.

"Hey girl, you okay?"

I turned around to face Pilar who stood at the threshold of my room with a bottle of wine in one hand, and two wine goblets in the other. "Not only am I okay, but I think I'm going to get even better. What have you got there?"

"A bottle of pure gold from Blooms Winery—you know, where we went wine tasting a few months ago?" And holding the two glasses out to me, she said, "You interested?"

"Heck yeah. It's not often I would even think of drinking in the middle of the day, but I'll make an exception this one time. Can we sit out on the deck? Oh! And I brought some sourdough and bruschetta with me. I'll put together a plate for us and we can pretend we're retired and haven't a care in the world."

"Sounds like a plan. You know your way around the kitchen, so get to it and I'll grab the wine opener and meet you out on the deck."

. . . . .

I enjoyed how it felt to push my cares behind me with the help of a good friend and a fabulous bottle of wine. "I can't believe we drank that entire bottle. That is—or was—one very good Viognier. Don't let me leave without buying a bottle, or six, from the winery."

"Will do. So, now that you're loosened up, tell me the truth. How long has it been since you picked up your knitting needles?"

After my husband's accident, Pilar hosted me at her Freeland beach house for two weeks while I licked my wounds and tried to figure out how the devil I would carry on without Allan. In between my countless naps and crying bouts, she taught me the calming art of knitting—something about which she knows quite a bit given the fact that she owns her own island store called *Peace, Love, and Yarn*. I kept at it for quite a while and even made a vest and a pair of socks for Dad—the latter of which he loved—and a doggie sweater for Ramona, which she refused to wear. Feigning ignorance as to why Pilar asked about my knitting habits I said, "Not in a while, why?"

"Because you're wound up tighter than a banjo string. I bet you haven't partaken of my panacea for all things stressful in ages, have you?"

"Ooooh, listen to you with the sophisticated vocabulary. When did you learn *that* word?"

"I'll ignore your dig because I love you and I know you don't mean to be a bitch, but I won't stand for you not doing what I taught you to do. Thanks to you, I've been jogging like a mad woman and managed to get a pretty nice-looking ass in the process. You, on the other hand, have not practiced what I taught and it shows in how miserable you look."

I crossed my arms and turned to Pilar. "I'll have you know I've been very busy. I work most days of the week, I help Dad out pretty much every day of the week, and I'm constantly dodging the snarky comments and opinions of my brother. That in itself has turned into a full-time job."

"I know things are real bad for you right now, but the knitting was supposed to be your Zen time like it was after Allan died. You once told me that sitting down to knit at the end of the day to create something for someone was better than a day's worth of meditation—not that you would know what a day's worth of meditation feels like."

"And you do?"

"No, I don't, but I'm not the one with crease lines on her face where none used to be, and hair that's twenty-five percent grayer than when I last saw you."

"Pfft!" I said in indignation.

"Don't 'pfft!' me. That's not geezer gray I see, that's stress gray."

I couldn't take it anymore and stood to my feet, pointing my finger at my best friend's face. "I've got news for you, knitting isn't going to heal my dad or wipe away all this—" I fluttered my hands up in the air in circles to come up with the right word, "This shit!" Then I plopped into my deck chair and bawled like a baby.

Pilar took my hand. "Hon, I know knitting isn't a miracle drug, it's just that I'm worried sick about you . . . and answer me this . . . when was the last time you had sex?"

I shook my head, shocked at the abrupt change in subject. "I don't think having sex is the answer for what ails me."

"Hush up, sex is always the answer."

Pilar stood, leaned toward me, and pointed her finger at me. "Come on girl, you need to get out there before you dry up." I followed Pilar with my eyes as she sat back down in her Adirondack chair with a self-satisfied look on her face.

"Okay my friend, which is it, knitting or sex that's the cure-all, huh?"

"Who says you hafta choose? But seriously, you need the kind of help over there in Seattle that I can't give you." Pilar jumped up. "Hold on a sec."

She returned with two tall glasses of water, her reading glasses, and a sheaf of papers. Colleen accepted a glass. "Thanks for the water, if I'm going to avoid a hangover I'd better hydrate." I gulped my entire glass and started in on Pilar's.

Pilar waved the papers in front of Colleen. "Now look here at what I've got. Ya' know, when I'm not too busy at work I get on my Mac and do research for you. I searched for groups that help people like you and came across the Alzheimer's Association website. Did you know they offer support group meetings, and they're free?"

She didn't wait for my answer. "The meetings are all over the place. I found one that's kind of in between where you live and where you work. It's at the Midtown Senior Center on Monday afternoons."

"I don't know, that's one of my days off and I usually spend a good part of the day going on errands with Dad, you know, taking him to doctor appointments and stuff. I don't think that would work out for me, and besides, we don't even know for sure if Dad has Alzheimer's."

Pilar slapped the papers on her lap. "I can't believe what I'm hearing. This support meeting stuff is exactly what you need and you're turning up your nose at it. Hon, you can stay at my house any time you want, you can call me as many times a day as you need to, but I'll never have all the right things to say to you because I've never experienced what you're experiencing."

Pilar laid out the papers on her lap and put on her reading glasses. "And besides, it says right here, 'Alzheimer's Association support groups provide a consistent and caring place for people to learn, share and gain emotional support from others dealing with Alzheimer's or a related dementia.' Your dad doesn't even have to have Alzheimer's to qualify, right now he falls into the 'a related dementia' category."

Pilar placed the information on the table between us. "Won't you at least look into it? It's only an hour and a half out of your precious Monday so you'd still have plenty of time to spend with your dad." Then looking at me with doleful eyes, she added the clincher, "Do it for me, please?"

I picked up the papers and rolled them up. "See, this is why we're such good friends: you always make me feel better, and you care enough about me to yell at me. I'll look into it when I get back to Seattle, but right now, I need to pee real bad and then I want us to take the dogs on a walk."

I headed into the house at a fast clip but could still hear Pilar yelling at me. "Sounds good to me, but tomorrow morning you and I are going jogging so I can show you how proficient I've become at pounding the ground with my Nikes." Then I heard her say, "How do you like that word? Proficient!"

I laughed at that one and felt guilty at the same time. How am I going to tell Pilar I haven't jogged in a while either? I'm toast.

FIVE

Dad and I had a few items to pick up at the store so after our Sunday visit with Mom, we headed to the local mega-grocery store. "Let's pick up those toiletry items you said you were almost out of and I can get the veggies I need for a new recipe I'm making tonight. It won't take very long, I know you want to get to your Sunday paper."

"The paper? Oh yes, it's Sunday so I have a large newspaper to read. Don't rush on my account, it can wait."

"Well, I know it can wait but not for very long. You still enjoy reading the paper, don't you?"

"What's that?"

"The newspaper."

"Of course."

I was in luck, there was a parking space not too far from the entrance so I grabbed it before any other shopper noticed the great find. With the back-to-school sales in full force, I thought for sure I'd end up in what I call "The Back 40" of the store's parking lot. I secured the parking brake, threw my purse over my shoulder and rushed over to the passenger side to see if Dad needed any help getting out of the car. Nope, not this time.

As we entered the store, I picked up a hand basket from the entry way. "Let's head to the toiletry aisle first so we can get that bath soap and shampoo you like. How's that sound?"

Dad grabbed my free hand. "Let's go!"

I placed a four-pack of bath soap in the basket and eyed the baby shampoo at the end of the aisle. "Dad, you stay here while I get your shampoo, I'll be quick."

I let go of his hand, picked up a couple items that I needed in the same aisle, grabbed the shampoo, and tossed it in the basket. I turned back towards where I left Dad. "Ready or not, here I come." But he wasn't where I left him; in fact, he was nowhere in sight.

"Come on Dad, where'd you go?" I walked to the next aisle; not there. I then rushed to another aisle over; no luck. I couldn't believe an old guy like my dad could move so fast. He wasn't anywhere nearby and I didn't know whether to go left to the housewares section, or right to the grocery section. Fortunately a store employee noticed my distress and asked if she could help.

After giving my dad's name and physical description to the employee, she and I split up, both going in opposite directions shouting, "Dad!" and "Patrick!" as we searched the aisles. I made it to the produce section when I heard an announcement, "Colleen Strand, please report to the Customer Service Desk at the front of the store."

I left my basket of items on the ground in the organic veggies section and headed to the area of the store where Dad and the helpful employee stood at attention—both with a smile on their face and both giving me the "thumbs up" sign when I reached them.

"Dad, I guess I lost track of you for a while but I'm glad this nice gal found you. Sorry I left you alone, are you okay?"

None the worse for wear, he placed a hand on my shoulder, "I thought I saw someone I knew," and shrugging his shoulders he added, "I was wrong. Then *you* disappeared into thin air, but all's well that ends well."

Dad looked at my empty hands. "I thought we were going shopping, where's my soap and shampoo?"

The store employee agreed to stay with Dad while I went back to retrieve his toiletries and since I was already in the produce section, I grabbed a red pepper and a parsnip for my recipe.

As I walked back to Dad, I used that time to assess my current dilemma and mumbled, "Note to self: never leave Dad alone in a store for even a couple seconds. No turning your back, no getting distracted. Focus, focus, focus."

•　•　•　•　•

Colleen mentioning the Sunday paper earlier that day reminded Patrick to take last week's newspapers out of the plastic sleeves and mess them up a bit before placing them in the recycle bin; he didn't want Colleen to find out about his reading troubles.

He consulted with his wife. "As you already know, Connie, it's Sunday. Can't remember if I told you, the newspaper doesn't make any sense to me anymore so I stopped reading it. Started a couple weeks ago when I had a devil of a time following the stories. Well honey, try as I may, I still can't get through 'em. I'm not going to tell that sweet daughter of ours because I don't want to worry her any more than necessary. Since I can't read the paper, I decided not to renew it but I have to remember to cancel it."

Patrick snapped his fingers. "Honey Bun, I just thought of something, I'll talk to you later."

He went into his bedroom and grabbed the *Reminder Tablet* by the side of the bed and wrote STOP PAPER. "That should do it. Huh, that other reminder looks pretty old, I'm sure I've taken care of it."

He crossed off the notation for a future urology appt. "I wonder when that appointment is supposed to be. Oops, gotta see a man about a horse, sure hope the plumbing works better this time."

SIX

A day after losing Dad at the supermarket, I called Patty and with my *Dad Journal* open on my lap, the two of us went through the memorable incidents of the past few months. Looking at all the entries and talking it out with Patty helped to clarify things for me.

"So Patty, remember what you said about getting a second opinion about Dad's memory lapses?"

"Yeah, after he became confused when you guys visited Mom. Do you think that time has come?"

"I do. It seems counter-productive trying to decipher all this information we've gathered on him when there are specialists out there who could tell us once and for all what we're dealing with. I guess we could wait a bit longer, but why should we?" Sensing the seriousness of my conversation, Ramona jumped up on the couch, sat next to me, and placed her head on my feet.

"I agree, what are you going to do?"

"I'll call Dr. Barry and ask him to refer Dad to a specialist, most likely a neurologist. I can't imagine the doctor would be opposed to the idea. Heck, I hope not."

"Come on now, don't go looking for trouble."

"I'm just employing that big sister advice you've given me over the years: 'It's better to be armed for bear and hunting squirrel, than to be armed for squirrel and hunting bear' or something like that. Anyway, I know you and I would feel better having a more specific diagnosis and I think Dad would too."

I rubbed Ramona between her ears. "I suppose I should call Jonathan and let him know what's been going on. His input may not be very valuable, but I want to at least give the Big Kahuna a chance to weigh in on the issue."

"Good luck with that."

"I'm not all that concerned about broaching the subject with him. I mean, regardless of what he says, we'll go the neuro route anyway, right? But first I need to sit down with Dad to find out what he thinks about the idea."

"Do you think that's necessary? You've been such a support for him ever since Mom died, I'm pretty sure he'd go along with whatever you say."

"That might be the case, but I think he'd be glad that I took his opinion into consideration rather than just making the appointment and telling him afterwards. He may be eighty-four years old and getting older, but he still has a brain and a heart and I'm not going to stomp on either of them."

"Okay, I'll look for an update when it's all set up. Talk to you later."

"You got it."

SEVEN

Rather than talk by phone with my brother, I arranged for him to meet me at *Third Place Books* in the Ravenna area so we could get caught up with each other. It had been a while since I visited this bookstore so it seemed like I could kill two birds with one stone. As one of the rapidly diminishing independent bookstores still in existence, Third Place offers new, used, and bargain books which pretty much guarantees I'll find something I want each time I visit.

Even after browsing and picking up the latest Kristin Hannah book, I was still fifteen minutes early, and as is most often the case when I'm nervous, my stomach betrayed me: two bathroom trips down, hopefully none to go before Jonathan arrives.

Speak of the devil. "Hey, Jonathan, over here!"

My brother sat down in the chair across from me and without looking up mumbled, "Hey, Colleen."

"Um, do you want coffee or anything? My treat."

"I'm good." He's finishing up what must be a very important text, so I just sat and waited for him to look at me.

He slapped the phone down on the table and finally made eye contact with me. "So, what's going on?"

"I really appreciate that you're here. Um, I'm worried about Dad."

Jonathan acted all surprised. "What about?"

"I've been thinking maybe it's time for us to get a second opinion about his memory condition."

"Listen, a senior moment does not equate to a memory condition. He's eighty-two for God's sake . . ."

"Actually, eighty-four."

"Same thing. He's an old guy with an old brain, what else can you expect?"

I shifted in my seat and pushed my coffee away. "What I don't expect is for him to forget where Mom is buried and I don't expect him to look at the holy water vessel at the entrance to the church and not know what it's used for, and I—"

"So he had a bad day or two. Don't you have bad days when everything goes wrong?"

"Yeah, like today," I mumbled.

"What did you say?"

"It's just that I want you to realize that Dad's senior moments are happening more frequently and they're more troublesome. A neurologist could help us find out whether it's a bigger problem than his regular doctor indicated."

"Look, Dr. Barry is a good internist whom Dad's trusted for many years. If the Doc says he has age-related memory problems, that's all it is."

Jonathan shook his head and with that crafty smile of his, he added, "As usual you're overreacting. I honestly don't think it's as bad as you say."

"Wow, that's some denial you've got going on there. I hate to break the news to you, but downplaying Dad's problem won't change what's going on with him."

I decided to change tactics. "When was the last time you spent time with him?"

"Oh, so that's what this is about? I'll have you know, Melanie and I had him over for brunch not too long ago and he was as good as gold then."

"Wait, are you referring to Easter?"

"Right."

"That was six months ago."

Counting back on his fingers, Jonathan corrected me. "Five months ago."

"Okay, five, but a lot has changed since then. Patty agrees with me that Dad could benefit from seeing a neurologist and—"

"So you guys already made up your mind on this? Why are you wasting my time on one of the few Saturdays I've had off in months?"

I feel like a kid who's just been scolded by a parent but who can't stop herself from talking back. "I'm sorry to intrude on your precious free time, but you need to understand that when I'm not at work, much of my free time is spent doing stuff for Dad—or at the very least, worrying about him."

"Hey, you took all this on yourself. When he started needing a little extra help you were the first one to volunteer, so don't you dare lay a guilt trip on me."

I grabbed my purse and stood to leave. "I can't make you feel guilty, Jonathan, you should be able to manage that all by yourself."

I couldn't get out of the café fast enough. Once out the door, I glanced through the window and saw my brother looking right back at me from where he sat. I should have walked away, then I wouldn't have seen him chuckle and shake his head at me.

• • • • •

I brought dinner over to Dad's that evening and during our meal I filled him in on my concerns. Like Patty said, Dad trusts me, so he didn't have any problem with seeing a new doctor. He even said that if a pill or two could make his brain as good as new, he'd be happy to add them to his pill-minder case.

I called Dr. Barry the next day who agreed to process a referral to Dr. Gordon Nesbitt, a neurologist at the University of Washington Medical Center. That's the good news. The bad news is that the first available appointment for new patients was two months away; I grabbed it. At least he was on the schedule so we would have a better idea of what was going on with him before the Holidays.

I gave Patty and Jonathan phone updates, leaving a voicemail for my brother, relieved that I wouldn't have to talk to him in person.

• • • • •

Jonathan listened to Colleen's message just before leaving the office to meet a client at a property in the South Lake Union area. "Hey, Jonathan, it's Colleen. I made Dad's neuro appointment for the first Monday of November, just thought you'd want to know."

Jonathan knew his sisters would accuse him of preferring ignorance over knowledge and hell, they'd be right. He can't stand the thought of his father losing access to his brain. Jonathan did the research and knew how bad it could get, he also knew the same thing could happen to him.

He wishes Colleen had left things well enough alone.

EIGHT

A few weeks after my coffee adventure with Jonathan, Pilar and I were on one of our frequent gab fests and although I couldn't tell her that I had acted on her suggestion about looking into a support group meeting, because I hadn't, I did tell her that I was going to make a valiant effort to establish some sort of working relationship with my brother. That came as a huge surprise to her but when I explained myself, she saw the wisdom of the idea.

Since Dad's laundry bubble incident, Jonathan's wife and I have had lunch several times; in the process we discovered how much we like each other. It sounds lame, but neither of us made much effort to get to know each other all these years and now that we have, we've become good friends and confidants. And besides, I can at least show my gratitude to Jonathan for his excellent choice in a wife by inviting them both over for dinner. But Melanie beat me to it; she invited Dad and me to their place for Halloween.

After Dad and I got out of the car, Dad said, "Your brother's house doesn't look the same as it did the last time I saw it. Are you sure you have the right address?"

I wanted to tell him it's no surprise Jonathan's house didn't look familiar because it had been several months since he last saw it, but instead I said, "It's probably the spooky decorations on the front landing that make it look so different. Let's go ring the doorbell and say, 'Trick or Treat!' and hope they let us in."

I rang the bell and before anyone could open the door, Dad yelled, "I'll huff, and I'll puff, and I'll blow your house down!"

I turned to Dad, "Well, that wasn't very much in keeping with the Halloween theme, but let's see if it worked."

Melanie peered through the side window and seeing that it was us instead of the Big Bad Wolf, she welcomed us warmly into her home. Jonathan took Dad's coat and when Dad reached out to give my brother a hug, Jonathan soundly rejected it by offering him a handshake. Melanie, on the other hand, initiated a dad-hug which seemed to please Dad to no end.

After I poured the three of us a glass of wine from one of the bottles I picked up on Whidbey, Melanie gave Dad a wine glass of sparkling apple cider and we settled in front of the fireplace.

"Melanie, you have a fine home. When did you and my son move in here?"

Melanie didn't miss a beat, "Gosh, Patrick, I guess it's been five or six years now, but it sure feels like less time than that—"

Jonathan interrupted his wife. "Really Dad? You were here fairly recently, you couldn't have possibly forgotten the house since then."

Dad looked taken aback, searching for a way to respond. Just then the doorbell rang and he got to his feet. "I'll get it!"

The front door was visible from our vantage point so before my brother or sister-in-law could respond, Dad decided to see who could possibly be ringing the doorbell at that time of day. While he was away, Melanie and I scolded Jonathan and told him to start playing nice.

"I'm back, there were a bunch of kiddles on the front porch yelling 'Trick or Treat' with their hands out. I told them we gave at the office and sent them on their way."

Melanie and I cracked up but not my brother, he filled his wine glass, shook his head, and said, "Tell you what, how about if I answer the door from now on, I don't want the neighbors to think we're a bunch of stuck up loonies."

Dad had a good retort for that. "Absolutely, you wouldn't want to be thrown out of this fancy-schmancy neighborhood. By the way, how long have you two lived here?"

"Honest to God, you just asked that question five minutes ago, you already know the answer."

Dad took a sip of his apple cider and said, "Son, if I knew the answer, I wouldn't have asked the question."

Melanie followed up with, "Yes, *sweetheart*, if your dad knew the answer he wouldn't have asked."

Turning to Dad, she said, "Patrick, we've lived in this house for about six years. Can I refill your apple cider?"

Dad looked at his empty glass. "Not right now, thank you, but could someone point me in the direction of the little boys' room?"

Jonathan showed him the way to the loo while Melanie and I went into the kitchen to get dinner ready. "I'm awfully sorry my husband is being such a pill. He just doesn't get it, does he?"

"I'm afraid not. Every time I talk to him about Dad, he changes the subject. Don't even get me started about his thoughts on Dad seeing a neurologist."

"Been there, heard that. Trust me, I've tried to talk some sense into him but he refuses to take down that wall he's constructed between his unfettered life and his dad's health issues."

Jonathan cleared his throat loudly as he entered the kitchen and told us that Dad was back from the bathroom and seated at the dining table.

Melanie ladled the soup into the bowls. "Perfect, let's eat."

During our squash soup and hot bread dinner, Dad asked two or three times what type of soup we were eating. I'd gotten accustomed to his repetitive questioning in the past few weeks, but Jonathan had no tolerance for it, so every time Dad asked about the soup, Jonathan went all dramatic on us. He huffed out his breath, turned to Melanie, and gestured for her to provide an answer.

Even with just the four of us at the table, the conversation was pretty loud what with Melanie and I talking about my nephew's plans after high school graduation next year, and Jonathan trying to interest us in his latest commercial real estate deal. Every once and a while I glanced at Dad who sat silent and bewildered looking. I was pretty sure he wasn't able to track the flow of our discussion, but he didn't look too flustered, so I tried not to worry.

I zoned out while I was looking at Dad so I didn't notice that Jonathan had asked him a question. "Hel-lo, I asked you a question, shall I repeat it just like you always ask me to do?"

I dropped my spoon into my bowl and wished I could reach over and wipe that smirk off my brother's face, but he continued his bluster, speaking louder as if that might work better. "I asked you if you still get together with your war buddies for lunch once a month. Do you?"

Dad looked at me, and then at Jonathan. "Were you talking to me? I'm sorry, what was the question?"

"That's it, I'm done." Jonathan threw his napkin on the table and stormed into the kitchen with Melanie hot on his tail. She closed the kitchen door and whispered, "What is wrong with you?"

"Weren't you in the same room as me? It's impossible to have an enjoyable dinner with that man at the table."

"Well excuse me for being the connoisseur of the obvious, but *that man*, your father, is having problems with his memory. It's not as though he's trying to piss you off. Geez, instead of being so angry, how about showing a bit of compassion?"

Jonathan leaned against the counter. "Well it's very bothersome, and more than that, it's embarrassing."

Melanie had heard enough and before she brought the dessert out to the dining room she pointed a finger at Jonathan and said, "Honest to God, get over yourself."

NINE

Dr. Nesbitt's waiting room was a bit more crowded than the last two times we were there. There were quite a few patients my dad's age, no surprise there, but what was surprising were those who appeared to be in their fifties or early sixties—patients who looked far worse off than my dad.

"Stop staring, Colleen, that's not going to be me. Those people must be dealing with some other brain condition, see how young they are?" I wasn't at all sure Dad was right about that, but I nodded and patted him on the knee as though he was.

In this busy neurology waiting room you could tell who the healthy ones were because they weren't looking down at a magazine stuck on the same page. The healthy ones weren't asking questions over and over again of their loved ones and they weren't walking around the waiting room seemingly in an effort to get somewhere. No, the healthy ones looked like me, and relatively speaking, they looked like my dad.

A nurse opened the door to the waiting room to call the next patient. "Patrick?"

Dad and I looked at the nurse. Dad raised his hand. "Is it my turn? I'm Patrick Quinn."

Yes, it was our turn and suddenly I had no interest in hearing what the doctor had to say. As soon as the nurse called Dad's name I had a fleeting thought that maybe I was making much ado about nothing; perhaps my dad's memory lapses were just very strong senior moments. Right, and maybe I could package and sell those thoughts as *Denial in a Bottle*.

The nurse told us Dr. Nesbitt would be in straight away and that we could sit in the chairs at the small conference table in the corner of the doctor's office.

"How are you doing Dad, you okay?"

"Well, sweetie, I'm worried, but I think regardless of what the doctor says, we'll both be better off in the long run, don't you?"

"Yes, Dad, I do."

It had been two weeks since Dad's extensive neurological testing. Since the testing, I did my best to imagine the best case scenario, so this time I was armed for squirrel, not bear. That turned out to be the wrong tactic.

The neurologist carried a thick folder into his office and after sharing pleasantries, he sat with us at the round table. Before the doctor switched to the serious stuff, however, I told Dad that I would take notes so he could relax and concentrate on all the doctor had to say. "Please go ahead, Dr. Nesbitt."

"As you know, Mr. Quinn, you've gone through an extensive amount of testing. You had a head CAT scan just before Thanksgiving that showed normal brain atrophy—or shrinking of the brain—for someone your age. A week later, I interviewed you for close to two hours with Colleen present during the first hour."

Dad took my hand. "Thank goodness you were there with me Colleen. It meant a lot that you could take time off from work to keep me company."

"I wouldn't have missed it, and besides, December is a slow month at the bridal salon, the staff didn't even miss me." I smiled at the doctor to encourage him to continue. Damn, he wasn't smiling.

"Mr. Quinn, a week after that initial interview, you put up with me and my staff for five hours while we conducted extensive neurological and psychological testing—eighteen tests in all. So we've spent quite a bit of time together trying to figure out the cause of your increasing confusion and short-term memory loss."

Dad leaned forward in his chair. "This whole business has been very frustrating, and I know my kids, especially Colleen here, want to know how their old man is doing. And Dr. Nesbitt, please call me Patrick."

"Patrick it is. So here's the clinical diagnosis that I feel confident providing you at this time: diagnostically, the combination of impairment of non-amnestic and amnestic domains of neurocognitive functioning, and impairment of daily activities secondary to cognitive functions, meet the criteria for a dementia syndrome."

I put down my pen. "Whoa doctor, you lost me at non-whatic."

The doctor turned to me. "I apologize, let me put the diagnosis in layman's terms. The symptoms your dad has been experiencing—"

I held up my hand to stop him. "Doctor Nesbitt, please talk to my father, it's his testing we're talking about."

"I apologize, you're right. Patrick, the symptoms you've been experiencing very much lend themselves to a diagnosis of a dementia syndrome that includes measurable impairment of short-term memory and the loss of your ability to concentrate on day-to-day matters that are important to you. You also told me that you are no longer able to read newspapers and other publications."

I turned to Dad, "You can't read anymore? What about the Sunday paper, that too?"

Dad looked down at his lap, evidently embarrassed that I was hearing this news for the first time. "I didn't want to worry you. Are you mad at me?"

"Heck no, this is me you're talking to, not your son, it's just that this is a new development—"

"Well, not that new, it started late summer."

Note to self, make sure to cancel Dad's newspaper subscription. "Okay, four months, we'll deal with it."

Poor Dad, he loved reading the paper, it had been part of his Sunday ritual for such a long time. Now I knew that when I dropped him off at the house after visiting Mom, he didn't have that activity to look forward to; he had an empty house and nothing substantive to do to occupy his time. Damn.

Dr. Nesbitt opened the folder and pulled out a stack of papers. "Patrick, I want to go over the results from some of the tests you took. I think those will clarify the areas of greatest concern."

I picked up my pen, opened my notebook to a blank page and said, "Ready when you are, Doc."

"After I've gone over the test results, I'll give you my take on where you are on the Global Deterioration Scale, or GDS. That's one of the assessment scales used by the medical and neurological community to discern a patient's level of cognitive decline. I'm sorry it sounds like such an unfriendly phrase—cognitive decline—but where dementias are concerned, the greatest focus is the brain's cognitive function."

As soon as the doctor mentioned test results, Dad shifted uncomfortably in his seat. "Ya' know doc, I've never been good at taking tests, right Colleen?"

"He's right Dr. Nesbitt," and trying to lighten the mood, I added, "My dad and I are smarter than tests would indicate."

Dad held up his index finger and shook it. "You're absolutely right!"

The doctor didn't seem too amused, but at least Dad and I got a chuckle out of it. The doctor continued. "Let me assure you that these tests are different from most tests with which you might be familiar. Very few people get 100% on them. Patrick, the two tests that were most significant regarding your assessment were the word list memory test and the puzzle formation test. How did you feel about the word memory test?"

"To tell you the truth, it was downright frustrating, I wanted to tell your assistant to slow down." Dad whispered, "I think she read the words too quickly. How's a person expected to repeat a large list of words if they come at ya' so fast?"

"I'm sure it felt that way to you Mr. Quinn, I mean, Patrick. Most people who take the test make the same comment. What we were looking for with this test were the number of words you remembered shortly after my assistant read them to you, compared to the number of words remembered several minutes later. You recalled seven out of twelve immediately, and five out of twelve after some distractions were thrown in your way."

I felt the need to defend my father. "I could be wrong, but that doesn't sound too bad if, as you said, your assistant broke my father's concentration by asking him other unrelated things."

"Unfortunately, that's part of the testing criteria, a criteria that is fairly standard across the board."

"You're right, I'm sorry. I get protective when it comes to my dad. I promise I won't butt in again."

Dad laughed. "Likely story, why Colleen here is just like my wife, Connie. She always had something to say and wasn't afraid to say it."

Dad smiled and looked up toward an imaginary place. I brought him back down to earth.

"You're right about that, Dad, but maybe we'd better let Dr. Nesbitt continue." I gestured for the doctor to do so.

"Five out of twelve isn't a great outcome but I'm encouraged that you were still able to retain some short term memories. Coming up with five words means that those words were able to imprint on your brain. In advanced cases of cognitive impairment, patients struggle to retrieve even one word."

The doctor pulled out another sheet of paper. "Let's move on to the results from the puzzles you were given to put together. My assistant showed you an assembled 3-dimensional puzzle that provided an image of a star when put together correctly. She then handed you blocks with white and red colored triangles and asked you to duplicate the sample puzzle."

"Heavens, I didn't much like that puzzle. It looked so easy when the young lady put it together, but I struggled with it. I know I didn't pass that one. Your assistant seemed to give up on me because she moved to a different task. That was a wee bit embarrassing."

"I assure you that her intent was not to embarrass you but I'm sorry it felt that way. The testing procedures dictate a certain amount of time for each task so she was simply following the strict testing guidelines."

The doctor consulted his notes again. "For this particular puzzle, you were able to construct one point of the star, but were not able to complete the star by assembling the remainder. Again, even people with no perceived cognitive decline have difficulty with this puzzle. In your case—and combined with other symptoms you've described—the indications are that you are having some visuospatial struggles."

"I'm not sure what that means but does it have something to do with why I couldn't see the cheese sandwich I made for lunch the other day?"

I looked at my father. "Come again? When did this happen?" When Dad revealed this latest news, I'm pretty sure I experienced the very first time I've ever felt flummoxed. It didn't feel good.

"I thought I told you about that. I'm sure I did. Didn't I?"

I shook my head and turned back to the doctor. "How are the

puzzle and the sandwich connected?"

"Patrick, your vision wasn't impaired per se, but chances are you experienced abnormal visual discrimination. Normal visual discrimination involves the skill of using the sense of sight to notice and compare the features of different items to distinguish one item from another. Your cheese sandwich on the dining table didn't appear to be separate from the dining table when you looked for it. You couldn't see the difference between the sandwich on the plate and the table top. Question, what color is the table top?"

Dad scratched his head and turned to me, "What color is it?"

In an instant I had to figure out why the color of the table had anything to do with Dad's sandwich. I elbowed Dad, "It's a dingy yellow Formica top, kind of like those cheese sandwiches you make." He chuckled, so yet again my attempt at lightening the mood was successful.

Dr. Nesbitt held out his hands in front of him. "There you go. Now, back to the puzzle—a construction activity—your brain did not succeed in carrying out the correct functions to reassemble the star. You lacked the spatial ability to construct a 3-dimensional object, the puzzle."

"Well then it's settled, I just won't make any more cheese sandwiches and I won't try to figure out any more dad-blamed puzzles. Problem solved, right Colleen?" I couldn't offer Dad much encouragement but I said it couldn't hurt.

The doctor scribbled some notes in the file, closed it and pulled off his reading glasses. "You know, this visuospatial dilemma is something that baffles scientists and lay people alike. The unfortunate thing is that these incidents, particularly at your age, will most likely occur more frequently as time goes by. Until that time, however, I think it will be more frustrating than harmful to you, as long as this element of your dementia doesn't manifest itself in balance problems in the future. I don't want you falling down and breaking a hip."

I nodded, "God no, we'll have none of that."

I directed my next comment to the doctor. "Would it help at all if he used a cane?"

"There are two schools of thought on the matter. A cane can help with his balance, or it can cause him to trip. I'll leave that up to you,

Patrick. If you'd feel more comfortable with a cane, I can prescribe one for you. Medicare will pay for it."

Dad shook his head. "Nah, I think a cane would make me look like a feeble old man. Isn't there some sort of pill I can take to help me remember stuff better and see stuff better? They've got pills for everything these days, I mean, if pills can give a man a four-hour erection, there must be a pill that can help my withering brain."

I cracked up, and this time, so did the doctor, both of us apparently glad for the humorous interlude.

"I'll address treatments before we're done here, I promise. So far we've talked about the test procedures and outcomes, but not about what those outcomes translate to in more specific terms. The word test told us that your short term memory isn't at its best. You can blame that type of cognitive loss to the various memory regions of your brain. As I alluded to at the beginning of this appointment, such loss lends itself to being Alzheimer's related."

I stopped writing.

Dad jolted in his seat. "Oh Lordy."

My thoughts bordered on a more inappropriate word in response, but I held my tongue.

"The other symptoms—specifically the visuospatial ones—point to the presence of lesions of the occipital lobe and associated areas of the parietal and temporal lobes of your brain."

I tried to go back to my note-taking but couldn't keep up with the doctor so it's no wonder Dad couldn't either. "I'm sorry for being a wee bit slow on the uptake, but are you saying that my brain is messed up in more than one way? And what does that mean regarding the GPS scale you mentioned?"

"It's all about where the plaques and tangles attach themselves, and without exception, plaques and tangles are not a welcome visitor to anyone's brain."

Dad placed one of his hands on top of his head, and the other on his forehead and declared, "Out damned spot!"

I giggled, not really feeling it, but I was impressed that my dad could still be so cute after hearing that he had a pile of stuff wrong with his brain. Oops, the doctor was still talking; time to refocus.

". . . Correct. Regarding the GDS scale, I would place you between

3 and 4. Technically, you're at the tail end of the Mild Cognitive Impairment stage, abbreviated as MCI, but you could remain there for some time before entering the more advanced stages of dementia. You might be able to enjoy this status quo without much noticeable change."

With that statement, the doctor placed his hands on top of the folder and looked at us with what he must have thought was an encouraging smile, but Dad and I didn't give off any encouraging vibes in response.

"I hope once you've been able to digest all this information you'll agree that it's better to know what we're dealing with—from a treatment perspective—than being in the dark about your condition."

"I'm all for knowing what's what, but how am I supposed to handle two dementias if I can't even handle one?"

I agreed with Dad. "Dr. Nesbitt, give us something to hold onto here."

"This is where the treatment aspect comes in. Patrick, I would like to start you on a very common drug that is prescribed for patients in the early stages of Alzheimer's. Cholinesterase inhibitors are the current mainstay for treating the thinking and memory changes in Alzheimer's. Now is the best time to start you on that type of drug, and assuming you don't experience any adverse side effects, we'll keep you on that medication on a go-forward basis."

"So that's it? A pill is going to be my dad's cure-all?"

Dr. Nesbitt seemed to look for some advanced wisdom in the closed file folder on his desk; unfortunately there was none to be found. "I want to be painfully clear about this with both of you. There is no cure for Alzheimer's. The best we can do right now is treat the symptoms and possibly slow down its progression. There is one other option, although you don't currently meet the criteria. On an ongoing basis, the University of Washington conducts clinical drug trials for Alzheimer's and other dementia. If you're interested, I'll place you in the database for future trials for which you might meet the criteria."

At this point, Dad and I were so overwhelmed, neither of us could utter a word, and Dr. Nesbitt seemed to sense the maximum-information-absorption stage at which we had arrived. "How about I explain how the cholinesterase inhibitor works and what side-effects you might experience while taking it. Once I've given you that information, you can get back to me with what you'd like to do. I can't force you to take my advice, I'd just like to be certain that you understand the pros and cons of the treatments I'm suggesting so that you can make an informed decision."

•   •   •   •   •

That evening, Dad and I cooked take-and-bake pizza at his house and went over the Global Deterioration Scale brochure the doctor gave us. We decided that being between the third and fourth stage of a seven stage disease wasn't the worse thing in the world since he was nowhere near the real nasty stuff towards the end of the scale. For Dad's sake, I skimmed over that potential depiction of Dad's future, telling him that we'd cross that bridge if and when we got there.

Above all else, I reminded him that the decision to take a new medication—or even a doctor's medical advice—was his to make and I would support him one hundred percent. I just hoped that in my efforts to help Dad maintain his autonomy and dignity, I didn't end up placing too much pressure on him.

Before I left, Dad gave me the latest version of his Advanced Health Care Directive and asked me to review it with Jonathan and Patty to determine if anything more needed to be added to clarify his just-before-he-kicked-the-bucket wishes. That alone convinced me he was well aware of the seriousness of his multi-part dementia.

After I returned home and took Ramona for her end-of-day potty walk, I called my best friend. "Pilar, tell me again where that Alzheimer's support group meets? I think it's time I get that extra help you and I talked about."

TEN

"Hi, I'm Colleen Strand. My dad, Patrick Quinn, was recently diagnosed with what his doctor says is mixed dementia. It looks like he has Alzheimer's and some other type that affects his visuospatial abilities."

I took a sip from my water bottle. "You see, two weeks ago, my dad and I attended the neuro-testing *reveal* appointment. The good news is we both live in Seattle. I wouldn't have wanted Dad to be alone when he was told that Alzheimer's wasn't curable. Don't get me wrong, I pretty much knew that already, but having a specialist say it to us made it feel like dad had just been handed a death sentence. Well, he had been."

That's as far as I got in my story before I fell apart in front of the group of strangers. Up until then, my dog and Pilar were the only ones who had witnessed my crying jags.

I looked up from the table at which the others were seated and saw faces that looked as sad as I felt; hell, the two older ladies were crying and they didn't appear in a hurry to mop up their tears. I looked at the meeting facilitator, who is also the senior center's social worker, and gave him a look that asked, "Now what do I do?" But I didn't have to do a thing. One of the older ladies moved to the empty chair next to me and put her arms around me, soundlessly giving me permission to say what I felt without criticism.

Then she said the words that made my day. "You know, sweetie, you don't have to do this all by yourself."

Up until that point, I hadn't interacted with anyone who truly understood what I was going through as the primary caregiver for my dad. The peripheral support I received from Pilar, Patty, and Melanie was helpful and very much appreciated, but even they could never grasp what it meant to be on-call 24/7.

I wiped my eyes, honked into a tissue. "Did any of you ever feel that you didn't have a choice as a caregiver—you know, it's either you or no one else?"

A young woman across from me slapped her hand on the table. "Hell yeah, I feel that way because it *is* me and no one else. My sister won't lift a damn finger to help our dad, says she can't stand the sight of him. Like it's any easier for me."

I didn't know what to say, I sure didn't know anything about her family situation. I looked around the table. A woman about my age spoke up. "I think that's the case for some, but not everyone. My husband helps me out with my sister so it's kind of a team effort."

I figured I kind of lived in a combination of those two women's experiences. I scrunched up my Kleenex. "I have a brother who lives nearby, but he hasn't stepped up to the plate. I also have some good emotional support from others, so I'm not completely alone."

The younger woman who had made the outburst said, "Lucky you." She then slid down in her chair and crossed her arms over her chest.

I felt bad about bringing up the topic so I tried to deflect the attention away from me. "Well, look at me, a newbie hogging the meeting. I'm glad I'm here, and Mike, I'm grateful that you called me back to tremind me about today's meeting, but I also want to hear what's going on with the rest of you."

I turned to the woman next to me who had extended such a comforting hug when I told everyone my story. "What's your name? Does your dad have Alzheimer's too?"

That drew a laugh from the entire group, especially the hugger next to me. "Oh my, that's very kind of you but I think you need to get your eyes examined. I'm Victoria Dawson and my *husband* has Alzheimer's." She placed her hand on mine and added, "A mixed up one like your dad's. We're in our eighties and my George is at the point where the only time he lets me out of his sight is when he's talking to himself in the mirror."

The other older woman in the group said, "Oh yes, Victoria, tell Colleen about George Two, she'll get a kick out of that."

"Mary's right, it is somewhat humorous. You see, George discovered a new friend—that's the George Two my friend here mentioned. I tell you, my husband can stand in front of a mirror and pontificate for an hour at a time. His favorite topic is gardening and he's always telling the other George what types of fertilizer to use, when to plant seeds . . . heavens, he goes on and on. But you know what Colleen?"

I blew my nose again, "What?"

"George Two calms him down and makes him happy. If my husband of fifty years can be happy while still having this god-awful disease, then I'm willing to cover every inch of our house with mirrors if it'll make him happy."

She put her hand over her mouth, shook her head, and added, "I just hope it doesn't come to that." She then retrieved a pen from her handbag, wrote her phone number on a slip of paper and handed it to me, and said I could call her any time I wanted. She then surrendered the floor to Mary.

"I'm Mary and my husband William is pretty far gone in his dementia. He lives in the memory care unit of the senior community where I live as an independent resident. I knew William was heading towards trouble when he kept thinking I was dead and didn't want to be in the same room as a dead person . . . me." Mary cupped both hands around her mouth and leaned into the center of the table, "I'll have you know that didn't do very much for my self-esteem."

She leaned back in her chair. "It took me a while to come to the realization that it was the disease talking, not William, but it's difficult not to hear your husband say those words when they come out of *his* mouth."

The meeting facilitator, Mike Valentine, turned to Mary. "Does William still sleep during the day and wander around at night?"

"Yes, he's still on that schedule, all the more reason why it was a good decision to move him out of our independent-living apartment. I can't imagine trying to handle that type of sleeping schedule long-term while still trying to function during the day. It was getting pretty rough there for a while."

A good looking guy in his late forties or early fifties spoke next. "I'm glad you're here Colleen, I know what it feels like to be overwhelmed. I'm Eddie, and my wife Katherine has early onset Alzheimer's. We're both in our fifties, so it was a real shocker when her forgetfulness turned out to be something far worse."

He rubbed his hand back and forth across his forehead. "I was shooting from the hip for a long time, thinking, 'I'm the husband, I'm the man of the house, I don't need anyone's help.'"

The other guy in the group said, "How'd that work for ya'?"

"You know the answer to that, Frank, it was crap. I fumbled around so much trying to help my wife—not knowing what the hell I was doing—that it caused her added stress. Let me explain."

Eddie slid to the front of his seat and leaned his elbows on the table. "My wife's type of dementia has pretty much affected her entire behavior. She used to be in charge of her own landscaping business and was admired by her employees because of her easy-going, complementary management style. She had to turn the business over to our son, Richard, because she went off on the employees, and unfortunately, some of the clients. And Katherine yells at me a lot— she uses some pretty colorful language at times—but it can't be pleasant being her . . . as she so often tells me. Life in our household isn't great but at least I got her some medical treatment instead of denying the obvious: she was sick, she was getting sicker, and I couldn't fix her."

I nodded at the familiar concept. "I'm acquainted with that denial thing, that's where my brother is right now, he's the family member I referred to earlier, but I'll save that story for another time."

The other guy in the group, by the size of him a body-builder of sorts, spoke up. "In my son's and my situation, denial isn't even an option. I'm Frank, and my son Sean is in his forties and suffers from the effects of a traumatic brain injury, or TBI. My son's one of the awesome service people dedicated to serving our country. He was in Afghanistan—second tour of duty—when an improvised explosive device, you know, an IED, went off while his convoy was patrolling the area. Most of his fellow soldiers didn't make it, but Sean saved a couple of them, earning a Purple Heart in the process."

"He's a good man, Frank. You're doing a great job with him."

"Thanks, Victoria, but it doesn't always feel like that. I'm afraid I let my frustration get out of hand the other day, a day when I was pretty damn mad that life had taken a dump on me."

Eddie laughed. "Good one."

"Unfortunately, Sean was on the receiving end of my tirade."

Frank spoke directly to me. "This was the family plan before Sean was injured: welcome Sean home from Afghanistan at the end of his last deployment, retire from my job at Boeing at the age of fifty-nine, then my wife and I would do all the travelling we had planned for our retirement years.

"Instead, Sean's brain was rattled so much by the explosion that he can't hold down a job and he struggles to handle some of his own personal daily activities. I have a military big brother buddy come to the house two days a week to help him out, and I take him to a Veterans daytime program the other three days."

Frank stretched his neck from one side to the other and added, "Oh, yeah, also my wife left us because she didn't want to deal with a defective son—her words not mine."

I said, "I'm so sorry."

"Anyways, I had to chuck my plans to retire. I'm sixty-five, and I'm still driving to and from Everett five days a week, hating the job that I had planned on leaving six years ago." Frank yanked off his Seahawks cap and slapped it on the table. "But dammit, it's not Sean's fault, and there I went all postal on him, overreacting about burning our dinner because I was busy trying to help my son in the bathroom. I still feel pretty frigging guilty right now. Boy did I blow it."

The other guy, Eddie, put his hand on Frank's shoulder and squeezed it. "Dude, you're only human, I'm sure your son didn't take it personally, I mean, how did he react?"

"He told me he didn't like meatloaf anyway and was glad it burned. I guess he survived my outburst 'cause we ordered Thai food and managed to salvage the evening by watching a movie."

"See? No harm, no foul. You'll do better next time." Then Eddie picked up the Seahawks cap and slapped it on Frank's head. "Chill, brotha."

I was floored by the remainder of the caregiver stories. A woman in her late sixties takes care of her partner who has Parkinson's dementia. The woman close to my age moved her sister up from Portland because the sister's vascular dementia rendered her unable to manage her day to day life. And then there's that angry younger woman in her thirties struggling to provide care to her father who has some sort of dementia caused by a lifetime of alcoholism. That last one threw me for a loop. The father she takes care of abused her and her sister when they were children. I can't imagine her struggle, and I don't want to. All of these stories are of real people with whom I have found community because they understand my story and can speak to my kinds of issues.

I guess I don't feel so bad about my situation compared to those of the other caregivers.

ELEVEN

Thanks to the generosity of the bridal salon's owner, Sarah Mack, each year *Brides by Sarah* shuts down on December 23rd and doesn't reopen until the first business day of the New Year. I'm quite taken with her philosophy: she would rather not work during that period of time, so the staff shouldn't have to work either. As Dad and I have done the past two years, we're getting together at his house for a New Year's Eve dinner.

When Mom was still alive, my annual end-of-year tradition was to spend New Year's Eve and day at Pilar's house on Whidbey Island, a tradition started by virtue of the fact that I couldn't bear to be alone in my condo without Allan for that holiday. Pilar knew that throughout my marriage, my husband and I did it up big on New Year's Eve. Allan would put together a fabulous home-cooked meal, we both dressed up in our fanciest getup, we danced to some prearranged iTunes, and then capped off the evening by watching the Space Needle fireworks from our Queen Anne condo. So Whidbey was my New Year's location the first four years after my husband's death, but with Mom's passing so close to the Holidays, I started a new tradition of spending it with Dad instead.

When I pulled into Dad's driveway my heart ached when I saw him peering through the front window, no doubt anxious for my arrival. I was certain he had been standing there for the past half hour, if not longer. I picked up his mail from the street box before grabbing my dinner makings from the car and headed into the house. Knowing Dad's propensity to hug me straightaway upon my entering the foyer, I tossed his mail on the entry table and rested my bags on the floor.

His hug didn't disappoint. "Wow, that was quite a hug, I don't think I have a breath left in me."

"Don't be silly, my hugs have lost a lot of their oomph since I've been out of practice the past few years." He hugged me again and kissed me on the cheek. "I'm so glad you're here."

We just saw each other the day before yesterday, but I know time goes by slowly for him without the daily structure Mom's existence used to provide. I always complain that my days aren't long enough, and Dad struggles to fill the overabundance of time in his.

I did most of the dinner prep and pre-cooking at the condo so all that remained was to place the food in the oven at a low heat. After I washed my hands I peeked into Dad's pill-minder case next to the sink. From what I could tell, the appropriate number of compartments were empty since my last visit so I felt confident he was on top of his med schedule. After just one month on the Alzheimer's medication, I didn't expect to see any noticeable changes, and I hadn't. I hoped in time I could say differently.

Dad came out of the bathroom and sat in his favorite chair. I brought his mail to the loveseat where I usually sit.

"Oh, you brought in the mail. Can you look through it and tell me if anything needs attention?"

I sipped my wine and went through the envelopes, two of which had red-colored "Last Notice" notations on the front. "Oops, I hope these aren't what I think they are."

They were.

"Dad, the electric and gas bills are past due. Um, did you receive bills prior to these?"

Dad took the two colorful statements from me. "I'm not sure."

Dad joined me on the loveseat to have a look. "I don't remember paying them but I must have. You know, I bet that snow we had just before Christmas slowed down the mail a bit. They must not have received my check yet." Dad shook his head side to side and sat back. "Used to be the mail always arrived at its destination, I guess not anymore."

I took a closer look at the bills. "Yowza, there wasn't any snow back in October and the electricity bill hasn't been paid since then." I flipped open the other bill, "Ditto with the gas bill."

"Well I'll be, I guess I *did* forget. Ya' know, your mother was the one who sorted through the mail, made sure the bills were paid, and balanced the checkbook. I'm not too good with those kinds of details."

He leaned into me, "Are they gonna shut down the utilities? Is my goose cooked? By the way, when's our roast chicken dinner gonna be ready?"

I rifled through the remaining envelopes and saw a "2nd Notice" on the Waste Management bill. "Dad, I think it might be a good idea to let me help pay your bills."

"Nonsense Colleen, I have plenty of money, you don't need to chip in."

I laughed and patted Dad on the knee. "What I meant was, I can start monitoring your bills and paying them from your bank account. Tell you what, you get the mail from your mailbox throughout the week, and after we visit Mom on Sundays we'll sit down together and decide what needs to be done. You can tell me what to do, and I'll carry out your instructions."

"You'd do that for me?"

"Yep, and a whole lot more."

"I'm ashamed you found out I let some bills go and that you now have to help out your old man."

"It's really no biggie. Look, this has never happened before, so if you ask me you should feel proud of the excellent record you maintained for lots and lots of years."

"Ya' know, sweetie, I can feel it happening."

"What's that?"

"It's like my head is stuffed with mismatched words and broken memories and when I try to make sense of things, it doesn't work like it used to. I know when you start to get older, some of that is a wee bit normal, but I think I'm beyond that normal stage."

Dad patted my hand. "I guess that new drug the Doc put me on isn't doing the trick, maybe I should stop taking it."

"That's your decision to make but I don't think you've given it sufficient time to be in your system to do what it's supposed to do. Are you feeling any different from a side effect standpoint? You're not growing any extra toes are you?"

He looked down at his feet, "Gosh, I don't think so. Help me off with these socks, will ya?" Seeing the shocked look on my face he shouted, "Gotcha!"

"Yes you did, come on, let's have dinner."

After a scrumptious meal of roasted chicken, red potatoes, and Dad's favorite vegetable—God help me, canned cream corn—we each feasted on a slice of warm apple pie. Dad topped his piece with a slice of extra sharp cheddar cheese, and I graced mine with a scoop of French vanilla ice cream. We sat side by side on the loveseat to watch the New Year's Eve Times Square celebration at nine our time—Dad barely awake to notice—and when the east coast celebration ended I loaded up my car with my glass casserole pans, Dad's laundry bag, and a grocery bag full of several weeks' worth of mail that I planned on examining at home. As I left his house for the last time that year, I talked to the heavens and asked for a bit of a break in the new year. Hopefully my plea didn't fall on deaf ears.

TWELVE

After reviewing all of Dad's bills and financial obligations, it made sense to take my monitoring of his finances a few steps farther than initially planned. Changing the mailing address of the utility bills was easy and once I created an online account for each of them I requested e-bills instead of paper bills so that I would be aware of each bill's existence and plan accordingly. Part of planning accordingly was to set up the bills for automatic payment from Dad's checking account. Taking that task one step farther required an appointment with US Bank to add me to his accounts so I could communicate with the banks as need be. That task was not without its emotional components.

I arrived at Dad's to take him to the bank and as soon as I entered the house he asked me to sit down. "Colleen, sweetie, I'm having second thoughts about this entire matter. Let's cancel today's meeting."

I treaded carefully on the emotional egg shells I felt were spread out before me and suggested we relocate to the kitchen table to have a cup of tea; fortunately I allowed more than enough time for today's field trip. To save time, however, I put two mugs of water in the microwave rather than wait for the pot to boil.

"Tell me what you're thinking. What's brought about this change of mind?"

Dad squeezed his lips together in a fine line, took a deep breath and exhaled. "What will the bank think of me, not being able to manage my own finances?"

The oven beeped so I stood and added a tea bag to each of our mugs to buy me adequate time to respond. Seated back at the table with mugs in hand, I ventured forth with some encouragement.

"You know, Dad, it's not all that unusual for additional family members to be added to bank accounts. Sometimes it's a matter of the account holder not having enough time or interest in handling the nitty gritty of bill paying and such. Just because I'll be involved doesn't mean you're a silent partner, and it certainly doesn't send up a red flag to the bank employees that you're a problem customer."

Dad blew on his mug, took a sip, and put it down. "I wasn't aware it was common practice for others to be involved in someone else's financial affairs."

"I'm not saying that most people employ such a system, but I am saying that it's not unheard of and it's becoming more and more common." I wrung out my tea bag and continued. "I need to know if you're having doubts about me in particular handling your accounts. Is that the case?"

"Mercy no. I have complete trust in you, haven't I proved that already?"

"I'm sorry, I didn't mean to suggest you didn't, I guess I just want you to be one hundred percent comfortable doing this and if you aren't we'll figure something else out."

"That's not necessary, I'll go through with it. It was tough coming to the realization that I was no longer able to do the bill paying like your mother did—and I'm not ashamed to say I lost some sleep over it—so it makes sense that someone else should take over those details."

Dad took my hand in his as a tear rolled down his cheek. "Please understand, Colleen, this is without a doubt one of the most difficult things I've had to do."

Strangely enough, I secretly hoped that was the case because I imagined numerous future happenings that would prove far worse than this banking task. "I do understand, and I take this responsibility very seriously. Everything I do for you comes from my desire to make your day-to-day life easier and somehow more enjoyable. I think relieving you of this mundane but frustrating chore will do that. Are you game? Shall we head to the bank?"

"I'm game, but boy howdy do I need to pee. Do I have time?"

"Take all the time you need, the bank's not going anywhere."

I cleaned up the tea implements while Dad took care of his business. Today's discussion helped me more clearly understand the toll this disease exacted from its victims. Caregivers like me needed to remember that the frustrations we feel pale in comparison to those of the patient. I kind of wished his disease would progress to the time when he would no longer understand what it was doing to him. That unwelcome thought came from Dr. Nesbitt's nurse practitioner who told me that through the course of the disease, Dad would continue to slide to the point where he'd eventually be content in his dementia. She called that "being blissfully unaware."

Bliss or not, I still wasn't looking forward to him moving farther and farther away from his dad-ness. I decided to act more proactively when it came to things he needed help with. If I could do that, maybe I'd prevent him from being aware he even had a need.

THIRTEEN

The month of January marks the opportunity to celebrate Dad's birthday which I promised to celebrate in whatever way he wanted. I knew I would see him soon when we visited Mom, but I decided to call him the day before because I wanted to confirm our plans for his eighty-fifth.

Ramona and I returned from our very brisk walk to Kerry Park, shed our outer layers—I finally managed to coax her to wear the doggie sweater I made—and I grabbed the phone to check in on Dad.

I turned to Ramona. "Now that's weird, no answer, and it's . . ." I checked the clock on the fireplace mantel, "four o'clock and getting dark."

His voicemail kicked in. "Dad, it's Colleen, call me when you get this message."

I figured he was in the bathroom so I gave him some time to finish that task, but fifteen minutes later he still hadn't returned my call. I dialed him again, and again the call went to voicemail after several rings. I grabbed Ramona's leash. "Hey, Ramona, wanna go for a ride?" Ramona was excited but I was worried as I struggled to keep within the speed limit the four miles between my place and Dad's.

When we arrived at the house, I saw him through the front window seated at the kitchen table. When Ramona barked a greeting, Dad came to the door and let us in. "Hi kiddo, what brings you here with your shaggy dog? Is it my birthday already?"

I gave him a hug and held him away from me. "No, you're still a young eighty-four, but Dad, I called you two times in the last half hour and you didn't pick up. Did you hear the phone ring?"

"I did, and I walked right over to the kitchen wall phone and when I got there I forgot how to use it. The second time it rang I was in the bathroom—I have to tell you I'm having a devil of a time peeing lately—and once I finished up and walked to the phone, I still couldn't figure it out. I bet it's because I'm tired. I didn't sleep all that well last night."

I took Dad's hand and led him to the phone to demonstrate its use. "When it rings, lift this hand piece, hold it to your ear and mouth, and say 'hello'. When the call is done, just put the hand piece back where you found it."

I grabbed my cell phone. "Let's do a dry run. I'll call and you answer the phone."

"Now why would you need to call me, Colleen? I'm right here. That's the silliest thing I ever heard."

"Just humor me, okay?" I placed him smack dab in front of the phone and dialed his number; it rang four times. "Answer the phone, Dad."

"Why don't I just turn around like this and talk to you face to face?" Ramona stood at attention watching the scene unfold and even nudged Dad's hand in her effort to encourage his cooperation. Dad turned back to me. "Let's stop this nonsense. Do you want some tea? I'll heat up a pot for us."

I gave in, put away my phone, and helped him with the tea. Seated at his dining table I pursued what appeared to be a new quandary which Dad confirmed after a bit of prodding on my part. His home phone, and therefore the voicemail system, were now beyond his capabilities. Apparently, for the past week he had difficulty figuring out how to answer both the antiquated wall phone and his cell phone, but thanks to speed dial he could still use his cell phone to call me. Go figure. That was a relief, but what unnerved me was that on days when I didn't see him, I'd have no way of getting in touch with him.

"Dad, what time is it right now?"

He looked at the old plastic wall clock above the table, "Five fifteen, why, are you hungry? You want some dinner?"

"Maybe later. Come with me to the bedroom."

We ambled to his room. "What time is it right now?"

Dad looked at his bedside digital clock, "Five seventeen. Colleen, if you're hungry, just say so and I'll open a can of soup."

I took him by the hand and seated us both on the loveseat in his living room. I faced him and said, "I need you to use your cell phone to call me twice a day, every day, so I know you're okay." I got up off the loveseat, grabbed Dad's cell phone that was charging in the kitchen, handed it to him, and told him to call me.

"Not this again, we're both right here."

My look of frustration convinced him to do as he was told and to my relief, he speed-dialed my cell phone without a hitch. "Good, that's what we're going to do. Will you agree to call me at nine in the morning and six in the evening every day, except days I see you?"

He placed his hand on my shoulder, "Sweetie, if that makes you happy, I'd be glad to. Now, let's have us some dinner."

After some tomato soup and a grilled cheese sandwich, I asked Dad to call me one more time as a test; he passed. I then told him I'd see him the next day and then I headed home. Both Ramona and I sat by the fire while I called Patty and filled her in on the latest. My sister calls Dad once a week, usually on Mondays, so she had yet to encounter a phone-calling snafu. She expressed as much concern as I had and wondered how long it would take for Dad to forget to charge his cell phone and/or forget how to use it. And it seemed likely he'd forget the nine and six o'clock calling times. With another support meeting coming up the following week, I told Patty I'd ask the group for any suggestions they might have regarding this latest speed bump.

·　·　·　·　·

"Oh Lordy, Connie, looks like I lost some more of my marbles today. I wonder where I am on that GPS scale now. Thank goodness our daughter is keeping an eye on me which I'm sure glad for, but I worry about her too. If you have the time—you know, if you're not too busy looking out for me—could you peek in on Colleen every once and awhile? Or maybe you could zap our son with some loving-kindness and get him to help her out some. You know, he's pretty much a no-show when it comes to these things. Thanks, Connie."

Patrick snapped his fingers, "Just remembered something else, how about you find a nice fella for Colleen, you know, someone like her Allan. If you could find someone even close to that son-in-law of ours, I know I'd worry less, and I bet that'd make you happy too. Okay, that's it for now, good night, Connie."

FOURTEEN

My brother's wife and I met for lunch the day after my support group meeting to discuss the various daddy-monitoring options. Only one person in the support group, Rose, had the need for anything remotely close to what I was looking for. Sophia, Rose's sister, can stay home by herself—kind of—but she tends to wander away from the house from time to time. Rose bought her a GPS bracelet that has an emergency monitoring arrangement that helps locate Sophia when she does wander. As far as I know, knock on wood, that's not a problem for my dad: he takes walks, meets with his Korean War veterans, and gets home afterwards. The meeting facilitator gave me several brochures on home monitoring systems, so that's what Melanie and I are looking at today.

"Oh my God, look at this one, an ankle bracelet. There is no way in hell I'd let my dad walk around with an ankle thing like this. He'd look like a criminal on house arrest for having done who-knows-what?" I tossed that brochure aside, and three others that didn't solve our problem.

Melanie scanned another of the brochures. "What about this one? Your dad could wear a wristband monitor that looks like a watch, but instead of a timepiece in the middle, there's an emergency button he could push. Looks like he just needs to be within a few hundred feet of the home base station—I would think you could put that in the kitchen or living room—and when Patrick pushes the button, emergency help is contacted. Let's see . . . oh, perfect, the monitoring people can talk to your dad, and vice versa, through the base station, no phones to deal with."

Of all the systems we researched, that one seemed to offer what we needed. If Dad had some sort of medical situation at home, or he fell, or he just needed help of some sort, at least this system gave him the opportunity to contact someone. I got goose bumps just thinking of the ramifications. "I can't stand the thought of Dad needing help and not being able to call me. Oh my God, Melanie, do you think this wrist thingy is enough to protect him?"

"I guess there's one surefire way to find out, and this is going to be Jonathan's and my treat. We'll get it set up for your dad, pay the monthly fee, everything. No fuss, no muss."

"But I should talk to Dad about it, I can't just let you—"

"Yes, you can, Patrick adores me." She huffed on the fingernails of her right hand, rubbed them on the front of her sweater and proudly added, "He told me so the last time I saw him, and although I'm not you, I'm not a bad substitute. Will you trust me to take care of this for you?"

I wanted to scream, "No! No! No! Me! Me! Me!" but I reluctantly agreed. I trusted Melanie, but I'm always the one who takes care of Dad; I'm the one who jumps into the middle of everything to resolve matters; I'm "in charge" when deciding what's best for him. Boy did I have a high opinion of myself, and that was something that needed to change. If it meant getting Jonathan to team up with his wife to do something nice for Dad, then I'd climb on board that bandwagon.

Now I have to convince my heart what my brain seems to know: I don't have to do absolutely everything, others can help too.

• • • • •

"Connie, dear, it's six in the evening and you know what that means, I need to call our daughter and let her know I'm alive and well and ready to raise hell. I'm also going to ask her to make an appointment with a urine doctor. I thought I had done that months ago, but no one called to remind me of my appointment like doctors are supposed to do—or maybe they did and I didn't answer the phone. Ah, hells bells, all I know is I've got to get rid of some of the pressure down there because I get up so many times during the night, I'm losing precious beauty sleep. It's probably nothing, but I'd better get it checked out."

FIFTEEN

Thank God I was able to get Dad to see a urologist the same week he told me of his issues down in the nether regions. I felt like a dummkopf not latching on to his comments over the past several months about the need to go frequently, or having pressure in the groin that was not relieved by going potty. A quick test of his prostate area—quick because it wasn't me, not so quick for the person being probed—revealed some swelling. A Prostate-Specific Antigen blood test showed a level considered somewhat high for someone Dad's age but not alarmingly high. And bless his heart, the doctor catheterized Dad in the office to relieve the pressure so that Dad's quality of life could improve before the antibiotic kicked in to treat what turned out to also be a urinary tract infection. I'm familiar with the discomfort of a UTI but didn't think it could happen to men. I was wrong.

I relayed all this news to Pilar a few days later, who yet again opened up her arms, and her home, to me. I told her I appreciated the offer but felt I shouldn't leave Dad at this time.

"I thought you said he was already feeling better?"

"That's true, but I'd feel more comfortable knowing that if anything came up, I could respond quickly. I can't do that if I'm on Whidbey with you."

•   •   •   •   •

In the end, Pilar convinced me to take the one o'clock Saturday afternoon ferry to Whidbey by reminding me that a) my brother lives nearby; and even better, b) my sister-in-law Melanie would leap at the opportunity to help out if Jonathan wasn't available. I remembered to bring my knitting needles this time, primarily to ward off any admonitions on Pilar's part, but I also needed her expertise on some buttonholes for a sweater that proved beyond my abilities.

With our dogs Ramona and Tristan reacquainted yet again and tuckered out after their afternoon of romping in and out of the water's edge, Pilar and I settled into our dinner-making routine that always included a bottle of Blooms wine.

I always enjoy the leisurely pace experienced during my Whidbey Island getaways. As of late, my at-home dining ritual has been a barebones exercise in throwing together quick and easy food that from prep to tummy is over and done with a half hour after I begin. Not today—it's six o'clock and we're still deciding which bottle of wine to open.

"I hear my phone ringing, I'll leave it up to you to choose the wine." I rushed into the family room and answered the call on the third ring from a number I didn't recognize. "Yes, this is Colleen Strand, who's calling please?"

All Pilar heard from her location in the kitchen after my initial question were bits and pieces of my side of the phone conversation. "What are you talking about? . . . My father was wandering around his neighborhood? . . . Is he okay? . . . Where is he now? . . . Can I talk to him?"

Pilar stood next to me with alarm in her eyes, asking me what was wrong. I waited for the officer to put my dad on the phone and told Pilar that Dad was currently a guest of the Seattle Police Department.

"Colleen, is that you?"

I fabricated a calmness I didn't feel and said, "Now what have you gotten yourself into, Mister? Did you toilet paper Mrs. Wilson's house again?"

"I haven't done that since I was a youngster, so no, I didn't TP her house or anyone else's for that matter. Ya' see, what happened is, I met with my friends at Blue Star Café for dinner, you know how I get together with them once a month. Any who, after dinner . . . I must tell you, I ordered the clam chowder, it was very good. You and I'll have to try a bowl the next time we visit your Mom."

I was frustrated with Dad's editorializing and tried to skip to the chase. "So, you had a good bowl of soup, then what?"

"Oh yeah, what was I saying? Right, we talked shop for a bit—you know how us old guys can get sometimes—and when I left the café it was darker than usual so things looked different than they do in the daytime. Long story short, I couldn't find my way home. It's usually such an easy walk, but I'll be darned if it threw me for a loop or two this time."

"Okay, so the officer told me you misplaced the house keys so you can't get back in the house?"

"Well, I wouldn't exactly say I misplaced my keys, I just forgot to put them in my trouser pocket before I left. Looks like I'll be spending the night in the slammer."

I was already half-way up the stairs to the guest room to pack and told Dad not to worry, that I'd call Jonathan and Melanie, and they'd make sure he could spend the night in his own bed, not the one at the pokey. "I'm glad you're okay, but the fastest way for you to get home is for me to hang up and call Jonathan to have him rescue you. Does that sound like a deal? Or would you rather rough it for the night and play a round of gin rummy with the prison guards?"

"Hee-hee, I wouldn't mind playing some cards, but I think I'll accept your offer of heading home if you don't mind. Here, I'll give the phone back to the police officer now."

While I packed my overnight bag, I managed to relay to the officer that my brother Jonathan Quinn or his wife, Melanie, would retrieve my dad, that I'd be back in Seattle later in the evening, and if there were any further concerns, they should call me. I called Jonathan who, thankfully, was available and willing to spring our dad from jail, then I stormed down the stairs to get Ramona's stuff. Pilar was waiting for me in the family room.

"I told you I shouldn't have come here this weekend. Because of you, I wasn't there for Dad." If Pilar didn't already know I was steaming mad, she knew once I started throwing Ramona's toys into her doggie bag.

"Hold on there. I heard you say Jonathan was taking care of it so why are you in freak-out mode?"

"You just don't get it, do you? My father was wandering around in his neighborhood and who knows what might have happened to him? I have to get to Seattle right now, I have to make sure he's okay."

"For pity's sake, Colleen, you're not God Almighty. You can't know all, see all and be everywhere at all times."

Pilar grabbed Ramona's bag in an attempt to stop me. "You're out of control. Jonathan is taking care of your dad, there's no reason you have to leave tonight, and besides, nothing bad happened to your dad. He's fine. Take an earlier ferry tomorrow morning if you must, but right now you need to take a few steps back and let someone else put out the fire."

"No, right now I need to do the responsible thing and get back to Seattle. Are you driving Ramona and me to the ferry terminal or not?"

She did take us to the terminal and we arrived just as the six forty-five boat was loading up. Pilar pulled over to the passenger loading area. "Please reconsider your plans, Colleen. Let me be the voice of reason in this situation and remind you that by the time you get over to Seattle I bet your dad will already be in bed. At the very least, he'll be good and ready to go to bed. Your arrival will just extend what you said must have been a very stressful day for him."

Ramona whimpered in the back seat, not sure if we were in or out. After a beat or two, I reluctantly decided we were in and would spend the night with Pilar and Tristan. We drove in silence on the brief drive back to Pilar's place.

When we got there and sat down with a glass of wine, Pilar tested the waters. "As your friend, I have to ask you a question that's been on my mind for some time now."

"Must not have been very important if you've thought about it for such a long time."

Pilar topped off our glasses. "Well, that was rude."

She gave me that angry squint she does sometimes and said, "Actually, it *is* important but I'm worried you may not like what I'm going to say."

"For God's sake, spit it out."

"Here goes. Why you? Why do you feel you have to be the responsible one?"

"Well, duh, I'm the only one available, other than my sister-in-law, and she just recently climbed on board the caregiving train."

Pilar leaned back in her chair. "Okay, I get it, you like being a martyr."

"I don't know what you're talking about. I'm just doing what needs to be done."

"Right, and because you always take care of everything, no one else has a chance to help out in your stead."

Pilar still didn't make any sense to me. "Like whom?"

"Melanie has already proved she wants to help, so ask her to do more things. And your nephew Kirby has a driver's license, right?"

"You can't possibly be suggesting that my seventeen-year-old nephew take my dad to doctor appointments."

While Pilar twisted her long red hair into a ponytail knot she said, "That's not the only errands you do for your dad. Kirby could pick up groceries, he could spend time with his grandpa on Saturdays so you have one less concern while you're at work. I can't think of everything right off the top of my head but maybe you need to sit down and write down all the dad tasks and assign Kirby, Melanie, or maybe even your brother, to perform those tasks."

"Jonathan? Pa-leeze."

"Yes, Jonathan too. Maybe he figures that his self-proclaimed Super Woman of a sister has it all covered so he doesn't even need to offer his help. It's worth giving it a try, isn't it?"

I drained my glass. "You're right—of course you're right—but I don't know if I want to surrender some of those tasks. Doesn't that make me look like I'm turning my back on my dad?"

"You won't hear me saying that about you, and I doubt anybody else who truly knows you would either."

Pilar poked me in the arm. "Well?"

"All right, I promise to try my best to delegate . . . but now, can you please help me work on some buttonholes on a sweater that has me completely baffled?"

"See? If you hadn't stayed with me tonight, you'd have no one to help you with your project."

I got up and went upstairs to drop off my things and to check my cellphone for any messages or calls. "Huh, no one tried to get in touch with me. Oops, I better call Jonathan and tell him I won't be home until later Sunday after all."

· · · · ·

"That was mighty kind of you and Kirby to bail me out of jail, son. I guess that was more excitement than you'd planned for tonight. Did I mess up your evening too much?"

Jonathan stood just inside the doorway even five minutes after letting his dad in the house. "No problem."

Meanwhile, Kirby stood in the living room with an arm around his grandpa's shoulders. "I'm glad you got locked out of the house, Grandpa, it gave me something to do tonight. I had a date, but she cancelled."

"Some young lady cancelled on you? I find that hard to believe. Maybe she realized she's not good enough for you and decided to let you off the hook."

Kirby smiled at his grandpa's words of support. "We'd only been on one date before and it was kinda all right, but I'm pretty sure I had more fun tonight than Shelly and I would have had. Thanks, Grandpa."

Jonathan looked on as an observer, pretty amazed at how easily his son interacted with his eighty-five-year-old grandfather. Clearing his throat, Jonathan told his son it was late and they needed to let his grandpa get to bed.

"Uh, Dad, make sure you take whatever pills you're supposed to take before you go to bed . . . Oh, and Colleen said she wouldn't be back in time to take you to church but she'd stop by and pick you up for an early dinner if you're up for it."

"Oh, that's fine, after today's excitement I could use a morning of sleeping in."

Patrick stood in the living room as Jonathan and Kirby made their way out the door, thinking how nice it would be to hug his son. Jonathan and his dad made eye contact, and with a final half-hearted wave, Jonathan shut the door. From the other side of the door, he yelled, "Dad, be sure to lock the door. As a matter of fact, do it right now while I'm standing here."

With a click of the deadbolt, both men walked away from each other, no closer to shortening the ever-growing distance between them.

•   •   •   •   •

Back home, Jonathan and Melanie sat on the couch and talked about the day's happenings. "So your dad survived his brush with the law?"

"I think he fared better than the rest of us. He always manages to look for the fun in everything. By the time I entered the police station several of the cops were gathered around Dad, shooting the breeze. He really made an impression on them."

"Of course he did."

"And you should have seen Kirby back at the house, he was so comfortable with his grandpa. He doesn't treat him any differently than he did before Dad started to decline." Jonathan put his arm around his wife. "I'm very proud of our son."

"He's a good kid."

After a few moments of silence, Jonathan bent down and rested his arms on his knees. "I blew it tonight."

"What do you mean?"

"I should have offered to take Dad to Mass and visit Mom since Colleen wouldn't be back in Seattle to do so."

He stood up and threw his arms into the air. "Ya' know, I thought about offering and backed out. God, I'm such a shit."

Melanie stood and hugged her husband. "You are not a shit, you're just feeling your way back to your dad, it takes practice for these types of things to come naturally."

Jonathan kissed his wife on the forehead. "It didn't used to. I used to be a good son, wasn't I?"

"You were, and you still are . . . wait a minute, that's not totally honest on my part. You're struggling with your dad's dementia and you haven't done a very good job of coping with that struggle, but you will."

Melanie kissed her husband and added, "But don't wait too long, you could run out of time."

Jonathan hugged his wife. "Don't I know it? I'll try harder, I promise."

SIXTEEN

I'm amazed at how I've come to rely on my Alzheimer's support group. Prior to joining the group, the people I complained to, or asked advice from, were limited to my sister Patty, my sister-in-law, Melanie, and of course, Pilar. It's a good thing Pilar's tolerance threshold for friends behaving idiotically is high, otherwise she would have bailed after last month's blow up. A true friend, and Pilar is a true friend, doesn't get offended when you have a combination explosion/implosion in her house. It's a comfort having sisters, friends, and fellow caregivers who understand what I'm going through.

When I walked past the senior center reception desk for today's meeting, Ruth-Ann, the Midtown Senior Center Manager, asked if I would show a new group member to the meeting room. "Colleen, this is Sergeant Dennis McGee, a friend of Frank's. He'll be joining the group today."

Whoa. My eyes, brain, and other parts of me took in the sight before me: a tall, fit man with salt and pepper hair, and a melt-in-your mouth smile that no doubt has served him well over the years. I hope I didn't make a complete fool of myself when I stretched out my hand to greet him. I recall that I smiled, said his name and mine, but beyond that I totally blanked out. This person is a fine example of the male species, and I don't normally say or think things like that.

Oh my God, I hope I didn't say that out loud. Luckily, Frank relieved me of my escort duties once the new guy and I arrived at the meeting room, so I made an attempt to calm down by filling up my water bottle at the cooler. I also reprimanded myself for acting like a teenager and reinstated my adult demeanor before joining the group at the table.

So much for that plan—the one remaining seat at the table was right next to the new guy so I held my head up and plopped myself down to his right. I instantly decided against small talk, fearing a droplet of drool might escape the remnants of my teenage self. Frank filled the gap by introducing the guy to the group.

"Hey everyone, this is Sergeant McGee—"

"Please call me Dennis."

"Sorry. Dennis is a veteran of the Iraq war and is the best thing that's happened to Sean and me in a long time. I already told you about the military buddy who works with my son a couple days a week." Frank motioned both hands towards Dennis and said, "This is the guy." A stream of welcomes flowed from the group. Eddie thanked the Sergeant for his service and I just smiled appreciatively towards him.

"Since Sean is at the Veteran's day program on Mondays, I asked Dennis to join us since he spends a good amount of time with my son." Frank took off his NASCAR cap and said, "How about telling the group what you do?"

"Sure. I started volunteering for the Disabled American Veterans, that's DAV, five years ago. Being a disabled vet myself, I wanted to give back to my military community."

Dennis saw a few of the members give him an assessing look. "I know what you're thinking. This guy looks whole, what could he possibly know about disabilities?"

Eddie said, "Busted, sorry. Mostly I was curious if you had to have some sort of disability to be a mentor."

"Good question. There are no written rules that a DAV buddy has to be disabled but it makes a lot of sense for that to be the case."

Then Dennis stood up, put his left foot on the edge of his chair, and lifted up his pant leg, revealing a prosthesis. "I lost my left leg just below the knee in an incident similar to Sean's, but in Iraq, not Afghanistan. Having an IED incident in common with Frank's son helps me understand him, and vice versa."

Victoria couldn't help herself; she gasped and then immediately apologized. "I'm sorry for acting like a Nervous Nellie, I am not at all squeamish about your missing leg. I'm just sorry it happened to you."

Dennis sat down and apologized for taking everyone by surprise. "I don't think about my missing leg all that much." Then he shook his head, "That's not true. Obviously it's a constant reminder of what happened, but I'm grateful I have the opportunity to support Sean and Frank because of it. In Sean's situation, there's no getting away from the fact that he sustained a life-changing injury, but restoring some of what he lost makes my loss count for something."

Frank gestured with his hands and said, "You guys, Dennis is being way too modest, I'm tellin' ya', the difference between how Sean is now and before Dennis's assistance is like night and day. Dennis helped restore my son's ability to do some of the mundane activities that you and I take for granted. Sean can do more now, and because he can, he feels better about himself. That's huge in my book. Dennis, do you want to tell them the types of things you've helped Sean with or should I?"

Dennis tilted his head in a sign of modesty, "You go ahead."

"Okay, here's an example that'll clearly paint a picture of what this guy has done for my son. After Sean was released from the hospital and settled back home, he wouldn't leave the house. I tried various tactics to interest him in stepping outside the house, but other than going to doctor appointments—with the help of anti-anxiety medicine—he preferred the security of being within the four walls of our home. Keep in mind, my son was an avid outdoorsman prior to his injury. He was an athletic guy who would rather play football than watch it on TV. Dennis managed to gradually build Sean's trust so that he felt safe being exposed to the outdoors."

Eddie turned to Dennis. "What did you do to build his trust?"

Dennis looked uncomfortable—like he didn't want to talk about it—but he did tell us the key elements he employed. "Because Sean was my sole responsibility, I could spend as much time as he needed to get better. It takes a whole lot of patience to help someone take baby steps, and an even larger amount of compassion when a person's spirit is beat down. Frank here does what he can, and I do what I can. Frank uses his strength as a committed father to help his son heal. I use my strength as someone who's been where Sean's been, therefore I'm able to discern when it's best to back off from therapy and just be his friend."

Dennis cleared his throat and turned to me. "You know, I'm just a guest, it's not right that I take away the regulars' time. Colleen was kind enough to show me to this room for the meeting. I'll let her talk so she can get what she needs from her time here."

I'm thinking, *Oh, I've already gotten what I need thank you* but instead, I gave the group the latest about Dad. His prostate, getting lost, and me acting out against my best friend pretty much summed up the whole pitiful story.

After I finished what I considered my shameful update, Victoria put her hand over mine. "Now Colleen, you shouldn't be so hard on yourself. At a meeting a while ago, I think Eddie said something to the effect, 'Tomorrow's another day, or tomorrow you'll do better' and I'm telling you the same thing. Sure, you blew your top but you put it back on, and now you'll be ready for the next time."

Victoria turned to Mary, "I'm going to tell the group the latest news about my George. I think they'll be interested, don't you?"

"Yes, go ahead."

"Okay, here goes. One evening last week George was in our bathroom brushing his teeth in preparation for bed and I walked into the bedroom to get changed. I took off my street clothes and brassiere, and was about to put on my nightgown when George walked into the bedroom, gasped, covered his eyes and said, 'Just a minute there, you're a nice lady and all but I'm a married man and I'm not having sex with you.'"

Her story is met with stunned silence, then I giggled, and Mary burst out laughing. Recovering herself, Mary said, "Oh my goodness Victoria, that's still hilarious," and then looking around the table, she asked, "Or is it? Was my excessive laughter inappropriate?"

Victoria said, "Not at all, it *is* amusing." Now everyone joined in the laughter.

"I handled the situation by telling my husband that I would sleep in the guest room and that he could sleep in his own bedroom—our bedroom. He caught me so off guard with his sex statement that it wasn't until I left for the guest room and climbed into bed that I realized the reason he said what he did was because he no longer recognized me. That's what's so disappointing, not being his wife anymore."

Mary disagreed whole-heartedly. "You hush up, just because George is confused about who you are doesn't mean you're not married. Listen here, William thinks I'm dead but I'm still his wife. That didn't change just because our marriage was erased from his brain. Mind you, it doesn't feel all that delightful, but I'm still married to him and that's what counts. Your role as George's wife is very relevant. I'm sure if he could, he'd tell you so."

With a forced smile, Victoria said, "You're right Mary, but it's just not the same. Fortunately that was the only time he objected to us sleeping in the same bed. I guess now he trusts me enough not to have my way with him."

Victoria folded her hands in her lap and turned to the facilitator. "Mike, you warned us a couple meetings ago that our names and even the nature of our relationship to our loved one may disappear as the disease progressed. I was figuring it wouldn't happen to someone who's been married for more than fifty years."

Mike started to say something but Grace interrupted him. "Not to be disrespectful and all, but I'm glad that most of the time my dad doesn't remember who I am." We switched our attention to the youngest member of the group.

"Just the other day I told my therapist that it makes my visits easier pretending that the man I visit isn't the one who abused me throughout my childhood. Besides, I don't spend all that much time with him when I go to the adult family home. Mostly I play checkers with one of the residents who isn't too far gone yet."

Grace laughed and added, "This other guy is hilarious. He makes up a new set of rules each time we play so I just go with the flow. He's a fun guy."

Mike brought up the point that what Grace was doing in those instances was simply going along with the other person's reality instead of trying to force the older gentleman into hers. Then Mike asked if the rest of us had similar experiences.

Eddie did. "Before I was enlightened about the benefit of white lies, I blew it with Katherine. I kinda had this self-righteous attitude that after twenty-five years of marriage, I could never lie to my wife and I was certain she'd never lie to me."

Frank shook his head and smirked, "Yeah, right."

"A-n-y-w-a-y, this was about a year ago. Katherine was convinced that we had vacationed in Maui earlier that year and I corrected her, telling her that not only had we not been to the island of Maui but we'd never even been to the state. I told her that she must have been thinking about our Las Vegas trip."

Kelly rolled her eyes. "I bet that made her feel good."

"Not exactly. She stomped her foot—a pretty common reaction on her part anyway—and told me I was an ass and that I'd made her feel stupid. That's all it took to convince me that I should have pretended that we actually had been to Maui, and then gone along with whatever story she wanted to tell."

Kelly nodded. "The first time I did that with Donna I felt silly because we're both in our late sixties and it felt like playing a child's make-believe game. But loving Donna as I do, I went along with it because I'd much rather create an environment that's more comfortable and less stressful for her. Doing whatever works in any given moment seems to be the key."

Eddie put up his hands in an act of surrender, "Trust me, I learned my lesson."

Sergeant McGee raised his hand, but Victoria corrected him. "Young man, there's no need to raise your hand to talk, you're not in school."

"Sorry. I gotta say, I'm super impressed with all of you. Sometimes military veterans are automatically given a hero's designation, and although that's very appropriate for most, after hearing your stories I think you're heroes too, and I bet those you take care of think so as well."

I finally felt confident enough to talk to Sean's military buddy. "I appreciate that, but speaking for myself, I can't imagine not helping my dad." Uh oh, here come the tears. "But when I think of everything he did for me, and put up with when I was growing up and even afterwards, I think being his caregiver is the least I can do for him."

I grabbed a tissue from the box that always makes the rounds at our meetings, blew my nose, and tried to avoid a scene I wasn't willing to have. Dennis put his arm around my back and gave my right shoulder a squeeze, then perhaps thinking better of it, retracted his arm and looked around at the group. That shoulder squeeze took me by surprise, but I was okay with it.

The facilitator added some closing remarks. "There's a lot going on with each one of you and I'm always impressed with how you adjust to your constantly changing circumstances. You've had moments you're not proud of, whether that involved raising your voice, correcting or reprimanding your loved one, or honestly wishing you weren't the 'chosen one' on this disease journey. I'm very proud of you and I agree with Dennis's assessment—you *are* heroes.

"I have a poster on the wall of my office that provides the definition of a hero: 'Ordinary people, doing the ordinary right thing, at an extraordinary time.' That's each and every one of you."

Mike then wrapped up that meeting's business with a couple announcements and he pointed out the new informational brochures he brought for that day's meeting: Caregiver Stress; Staying Safe; and MedicAlert® + Alzheimer's Association Safe Return®. I grabbed the last two, and so did Dennis, right after me.

Dennis rubbed his chin back and forth. "I'm surprised you didn't grab the brochure on stress, sounds like you had a round or two of it from what you told the group."

"I've got news for you, stress is a part of the job description, but I guess you already know that with what you do for Frank's son." Just to make him happy, I picked up the Caregiver Stress brochure as well.

Dennis picked up the same brochure. "Yeah, stress happens with Sean, but I think it's different when you're related to the person you're caring for, the stakes are higher, wouldn't you agree?"

I did agree. "But still, one could argue that your work with Frank's son also involves high stakes for you. I can't imagine that your post-IED experience was a piece of cake. You must still have residual fallout from that."

"That's true, and I appreciate that you realize that. I don't want to sound cliché, but I meant it when I said that helping Sean helps me too."

"I get that." And I also got that I didn't want this conversation to end.

He asked me out for coffee. I would have had time for coffee with the Sergeant if I hadn't overbooked my day, but between taking Dad to a late afternoon dentist appointment and doing his laundry while I fixed dinner for him, no can do. Darn, who would have thought I should have reserved an hour just in case an attractive and extremely nice guy showed up at the caregiver meeting?

Dennis offered an alternative. "I'm gonna assume that at some point in the future, you will have time for coffee. How about I give you my number and you give me yours, and in the next week or so, we try to connect with each other. Would that work for you?"

Yes, it would work for me, so we exchanged numbers and I rushed out of the senior center to get all my scheduled items completed, and I did so with a great big smile on my face.

• • • • •

My smile drooped a bit as the afternoon and evening wore on, however. I kept Dad company in the dental exam room but my attention was elsewhere. With a bit of separation from having met a nice someone—the first nice someone since my husband's death almost seven years prior—I experienced a sense of guilt that was not entirely comfortable. That same guilt permeated the remainder of my time with Dad to the point where once we had finished dinner, I couldn't get out of his house fast enough. I needed to talk to Pilar and I needed to talk to her pronto.

I'm afraid my best friend had yet another opportunity to be a part of a Colleen Strand meltdown. In very specific detail, I relayed the whole Sergeant Dennis incident from senior center lobby introduction to the exchange of phone numbers. Pilar's first response was to say, "Damn, he sounds fine!"

Of course I had to agree with her on that point but I couldn't get past the fact that Dennis was the one person who had any potential of being someone I could be interested in, and it worried me. A few organized group dating events in the past four years netted zero in the area of men who could hold a candle to Allan.

But back to my guilt, a guilt Pilar understood but didn't agree with. She is one of the few people I know who understands that grieving has no expiration date, but she reminded me that being with someone else doesn't mean the grieving comes to a halt; that allowing someone into my life now doesn't disregard what Allan and I had for ten years. As Pilar put it, "If Allan had been an asshole, he would have been easy to replace, but he wasn't an asshole, so your good-guy radar has been pretty picky, and that's a good thing."

It *was* a good thing, and believe you me, I hadn't been looking to get involved with anyone. I pretty much gave up on meeting someone like Allan, and quite frankly, didn't care if I ever did.

Pilar also reminded me that just because Dennis and I exchanged phone numbers didn't mean we'd be picking out wedding china any time soon. If I'd waited this long to be open to someone else being a part of my life, maybe this was the right time to see if I was ready. With those words of wisdom from someone who knows me well enough to dispense such words, I decided to see where things went with Sergeant Dennis McGee, and tried not to fret over where that might lead me.

SEVENTEEN

Miracle of miracles, when I suggested a conference call between my sister Patty in California, and my brother Jonathan, the latter agreed to hold it at his home rather than just participate remotely. That made me happy because my favorite—and lone—sister-in-law would be able to participate as well. The topic for today's call was Dad's inability to find his way home from a nearby café a few weeks ago. I guess my brother's direct involvement with that incident raised his concern level from zero to one point five. Since we're looking at ways to keep our dad safe should that happen again, Patty did research on the MedicAlert® system, and Jonathan and Melanie reviewed the extra brochures I brought to their house.

Patty chimed in first. "Hey you guys, I think this emergency system is a good thing to add to what you've already put in place at Dad's house, but I can't see him wearing two wristbands."

I looked at the band highlighted in the brochure and said, "I get what you're saying, Patty, but the safety at-home band he wears is like a wristwatch and this other one is more like a medical alert bracelet . . . well, duh, that's what it is." With that realization, Patty agreed it might work out, and she asked Jonathan for his opinion.

My brother took a sip from his beer and said that it couldn't hurt if we could convince Dad to wear two pieces of jewelry every day, rain or shine.

Melanie punched him in the arm, "Sure, he'll think it's jewelry if you characterize it as such. Look, the at-home wristband looks like a watch and he hasn't balked at that. I don't think adding this alert bracelet—or maybe we should call it an alert band—would upset him."

Melanie directed the next statement to me, "You're the one who has the most interaction with Patrick, how do you think he'd respond?"

I told her I thought he'd go along with it and then revealed my plan. "There's a brief video about the system online that I'm gonna show Dad," I looked pointedly at Jonathan, "Fortunately the video depicts a male person wearing the bracelet, not a female. Then I'll explain how beneficial it would be for him to wear it. If he were to get lost, an emergency responder—or a helpful neighbor for that matter—would know the medical condition for which he was wearing it, which would help them discern what they're dealing with and respond accordingly. Additionally, Dad's client ID number would be imprinted on the bracelet with an 800 number that when called, activates a hotline of resources to get him to a safe place. Jonathan's and my contact information would be in their system and be readily available without Dad having to provide it.

"We already know Dad doesn't remember our phone numbers so he wouldn't be able to relay that information to whomever was helping him. The mini-postcard I placed in his wallet with all the information anyone could need in this type of incident is what helped the Seattle Police Department get in touch with me so quickly last month. We were just lucky he didn't forget to bring his wallet with him that time, like he forgot the house keys."

Jonathan thought he had a better idea. "Even better, we tell Dad he has to wear it so we won't worry about him as much as we do."

I could hear Patty on the other end of the line respond very quietly, "As much as *we* do?" And then she added, "I don't agree that we make him do anything, especially using guilt as a prompt. Helping Dad with this shitty situation means treating him with dignity and boosting his self-confidence so he feels as normal as possible with such an abnormal disease."

Melanie agreed. "I think if everyone in the family follows that tactic, Patrick will be in good shape, at least emotionally."

I high-fived Melanie. "So what do you think? Should we sign Dad up after I've had a chance to get his opinion on the matter?"

Patty gave a strong affirmative and offered to have her and her husband Wade pick up the initial enrollment fee and the annual renewal fee. "We'll set it up so that the fees automatically come from our account. It'll make us both feel good that we can do something for

Dad and the family from our location here in California."

"Jonathan? You okay with what Patty and I have said? I mean, I think it'll at least buy us some time."

Melanie answered for him, "Yes, he thinks it's a stellar idea."

Before we ended the call, Patty told us that she joined an Alzheimer's support group not far from where she lives in Santa Rosa, and her first meeting would be Thursday evening of the following week. "What about you Jonathan? You should consider going to the meeting Colleen attends. She's certainly benefited from it, right Colleen?"

"I'm very glad I started attending, but Jonathan, there are other meetings . . . you know . . . ones that meet in the evening if you don't want to attend the daytime meeting with me."

Jonathan had the nerve to say, "Look, you girls may feel you need that kind of help, but I don't need a crutch like that to lean on."

Melanie couldn't believe her ears; she was fuming, and yet her husband—my brother—still couldn't help himself. "If I need any type of information on Alzheimer's, I'll find it on the internet, and besides, you girls seem to have it covered."

Patty left the call shortly thereafter, followed immediately by Melanie and I who abandoned Jonathan in his home office, both of us choosing not be in the same breathing space as the brute my brother had become. We both agreed that a glass of wine was in order so while we sipped on a Maryhill Rosé, Melanie and I put together a menu plan that involved each of us saving leftover dinner portions for Dad stored in freezable containers that we'd provide on alternate weeks: I would deliver meals on weeks beginning with an even numbered calendar date, Melanie on the other weeks. The plan was that Dad would heat the meals in his microwave oven on evenings when he ate alone. We hoped our family meal service would buy us some time before something more substantive needed to be done regarding his living situation.

Jonathan joined us in the kitchen. "Before you both get on me about my comments during the call, I'll relieve you of the need to reprimand me. I'm sorry for being such an ass, I promise that wasn't my intent. Colleen, I shouldn't have made fun of you and Patty for your interest in attending a support group. I think it's great that you're taking the time to do so, I just don't see myself feeling comfortable in that type of setting."

"Well, let me know if you change your mind. For the record, I definitely think you'd like the people in my group. There are three guys who attend. One guy is a few years younger than me and is a caregiver for his wife. There's also a guy in his mid-sixties who cares for his forty-something-year-old son who sustained a brain injury in Afghanistan, and there's also a Veteran who's helped the same guy's son get back on his feet. They're pretty amazing guys."

"Okay, I'll think about it." Jonathan grabbed a can of beer out of the refrigerator and added, "Keep us posted on the new alert system. I'm gonna go watch the game. See ya' later."

After Jonathan left the kitchen, Melanie put her arm around me. "Maybe he's coming around?"

I hunched my shoulders. "Time will tell, I guess, but I'm not holding my breath."

EIGHTEEN

Dad and I took a break from our walk around his neighborhood and sat in the shade to people-watch at Wallingford Park. When I was growing up, this was the go-to place for us kids to play. Between the multitude of climbing equipment for children and the lush acres of green grass on which to run around, you couldn't find a more probable place to find Jonathan, Patty, and me, any weekend or summer day.

"I gotta say, Dad, you're such a good sport. Thanks for being so patient with all the seemingly crazy suggestions I offer."

He watched the children on the merry-go-round with a grandfatherly smile on his face. "Look at those kids, they have so much energy, makes me tuckered out just watching them. Ya' know, I wish I saw my grandkids more often. I think little Kirby would enjoy this park."

Little Kirby? "Um, you're right. I remember when your grandson was lots younger and we'd take him to this park. Oh my gosh, he ran around and tried to play on each piece of equipment as fast and as often as he could. In those days, he got tired quicker than you and I ever did."

Dad looked at me and scrunched his eyebrows. "Well I'll be darned, I bet Kirby isn't so little anymore."

How to save this moment and boost Dad at the same time? "You know what? You're right on the money. Kirby is the youngest of the grandkids so he is 'little' in that sense of the word, but he's seventeen years old now."

I tried to get back to the previous topic. "So, Dad, since you've agreed to add the Medic Alert® system as part of my ever-growing safety program for you, we'll get you signed up today and when the new band arrives, you and I will secure it to your wrist. Question. Your home wrist band is on your left wrist, where would you like the new band to go?"

He held up his left arm. "Refresh my memory, does the new contraption look like this?"

"No, it's a lot narrower than your wristband with a metal oval plate attached to a very manly looking chain. Here, I'll bring it up on my phone again so you can see it."

I went to my phone's Favorites folder but before I could bring up the website Dad said, "No need for that sweetheart, I trust you. One of the guys in my men's group wears one of those for his heart condition." Dad slapped his knee, "Let's put it on my left wrist with the other one. Wait 'til Jerry gets a look at my double band get-up. He'll be mighty jealous."

"I'm sure you're right."

We spent the next ten minutes watching the kids play—and we got a kick out of Ramona trying not to get too excited while watching the kids play while she was tethered to our bench—and then we headed back to the house. I wanted to show Dad how to reheat one of the frozen meals I brought him earlier that day. He chose lasagna for tonight's dinner, one of his favorites, which is a good thing because two out of the five meals I brought for the week were just that. I sat with him while he ate, holding off on dinner since Dennis and I were meeting for dinner a few hours later.

Once Dad was settled in front of the television to watch a Mariner's baseball game, I headed home to improve on my wilting appearance.

•　•　•　•　•

"Connie, dear, when Colleen and I went to the park today, I committed another old man boo-boo. For the life of me, I thought our grandson Kirby was just a wee tike and said so to our daughter. I was gonna ask how old Colleen's daughter is but didn't want to draw any more attention to my earlier mistake. I wonder if our granddaughter is young enough to need a babysitter when Colleen goes on her date tonight or if she's old enough to stay by herself in the condo. I'm sure she'll figure it out."

"Oh, I want to thank you for helping Colleen find a nice young man. I haven't met him yet but she said something about him being in the military. I hope he isn't deployed any time soon."

NINETEEN

Dennis and I felt that our two coffee dates were quite successful so we both agreed to a longer time commitment for our next date: dinner at Pasta Bella, my favorite Italian, or should I say, garlic, restaurant in the area. I couldn't believe Dennis hadn't yet eaten there so I was happy to be the one to change his Pasta Bella virgin status.

I've always loved the Ballard area of Seattle; there's waterfront galore and lots of historic storefronts mixed in with hip boutiques. I discovered Pasta Bella by accident when my parents and I were playing tourist almost five years ago. The three of us were hungry for a very early dinner and this was the first restaurant that caught our eye, and our noses.

Dennis parked the car two blocks from Pasta Bella. When we were one block away from the restaurant we detected the garlic essence emanating from the kitchen vents. "You weren't kidding when you said to be prepared for the garlic experience of a lifetime, that's amazing."

I elbowed him in the ribs, "I told ya'. When we leave, we'll reek of the stuff, but it's a good reek, you'll see."

The Sergeant deferred to me to order for both of us so I started with the elephant bulb roasted garlic with a basket of hot sourdough bread to share. For his entrée, I chose the Linguini Carbonara with Pancetta, and for me, Gorgonzola Walnut Spinach Ravioli. If the garlic in those dishes didn't scare away the vampires, nothing would. When our plates arrived, I explained my restaurant dining rule to Dennis: half way through the meal we had to switch plates so we could savor both dishes. Dennis wasn't familiar with that concept, but being the virgin that he was, he again deferred to my judgment.

"My God, that was good. I didn't think I'd like a vegetarian dish but that ravioli was off the hook!"

I paused mid-wipe of my mouth. "Off the hook? That's not something I expected to hear from you, Sergeant McGee."

"Oops. In my work with a variety of ages in the DAV program, I've picked up a few phrases here and there. Usually I remember to filter my new lingo for the appropriate setting, but all that garlic must have broken down my defenses."

Dennis finished off his glass of Chianti. "And how come you called me Sergeant McGee? I prefer the more familiar "Dennis" unless of course you prefer to remain unfamiliar."

I apologized for my gaff and told him I would never make that mistake again and that I preferred he be familiar too.

"So how's your dad doing? I think you said you were going to speak with him about the Medic Alert® program today?"

"I did, and just like the accommodating and trusting person he is, he was on board with it. My sister's going to do all the online registration stuff at her end and I should receive the bracelet by Friday."

Dennis mentioned that it sounded like I had a lot on my plate and asked if I had anyone else to help out with all my responsibilities. I told him about my team that consists of my sister, Patty, in California being a shoulder to cry and/or lean on, my best friend Pilar, whom I victimize with my fluctuating moods, and my sister-in-law, Melanie, who does everything I ask her to do if she hasn't already volunteered to do it.

"And your brother? I assume if you have a sister-in-law . . . "

"Technically, I do have a brother. Jonathan is the oldest of us three siblings and wears that mantle like the overbearing, disinterested person he is."

"Why don't you tell me how you really feel?"

I toyed with the idea of ordering another glass of wine but opted to talk about my brother without additional medication. "Jonathan doesn't lift a hand when it comes to taking care of our dad but he's fast to criticize everything I do. I'm open to criticism—God knows I'm not perfect—but he doesn't offer any alternatives. What he does offer is destructive criticism that doesn't go over well with anyone in the family, including his wife. I don't know how Melanie does it 'cause she has to deal with him 24/7. At least I just have bits and pieces of him to deal with."

Dennis was silent. Perhaps he was considering all that I had said and was trying to weigh his words before responding; what a new concept, I could learn something from this guy. His eventual response was a good one. "I'm pretty sure spouses behave differently around each other than they do siblings. At least I assume they do. I'm an only child so the way I acted around my wife was the only way I knew how to act. Christine, that's my ex-wife, didn't have a close relationship with her one sibling, a sister."

"I figured you were married before. Is it okay to ask what happened?"

"It's okay to ask. I wasn't the responsible party to the divorce, at least not directly."

"Come again?"

"We had been married for four years when Christine met someone while I was on my third deployment in Iraq. She opted to be with a man she could see whenever she wanted, instead of just in between deployments. I found out the hard way, though. When I returned stateside my best buddy told me he saw my wife with another guy."

"No way."

"No way that my buddy told me, or no way that my wife was with another guy?"

"I guess both."

"Rob and I went through Marine basic training and two deployments together, although not that third deployment of mine. When you go through what we did, your life is kind of an open book. Your sanity is based on the connections you make resultant from those experiences. So anyway, Rob told me about my wife's unfaithfulness because he knew I'd do the same for him. We don't just protect each other on the battlefield, we protect each other off the field as well."

"I'm sorry you had to go through all that but I'm glad you're not still with her. I don't understand those whose commitment to someone extends to for better and for health, but not for worse and for sickness. That's a definition of a loophole, not a marriage. I don't think I'll ever understand that way of thinking."

"And that's a good thing." Dennis took my hand across the table. "It sounds like you and your husband had it good, I mean, until the accident that is." He squeezed my hand and added, "Sorry, I guess I stuck my good foot in it, didn't I?"

"Not at all. You're right, we had a very healthy marriage. We had lots of fun together and we talked to each other about everything: our hopes, our fears, our life expectations, everything."

"That's good. Christine and I weren't like that. We had a pretty empty marriage so I'm glad we didn't bring any kids into it. That wouldn't have been fair to them." He rubbed his thumb over the top of my hand. "And you and Allan didn't have children."

"You know what? We enjoyed ourselves so much, we never felt the need or the desire to add children to the mix. We travelled a lot as well, and we liked being able to pack our bags and go where we wanted, when we wanted. We didn't even adopt Ramona until we had been married for nine years, but I'm glad we did. She keeps me company when I'm alone and I swear, she's psychic—she senses my moods and responds accordingly. She's a keeper to be sure."

"I've always wanted a dog, maybe someday."

"Well, until you do, you're welcome to come over and see her any time you want."

"That sounds like a win-win situation if you ask me—two for one."

What's got into me? I blushed like a school girl and Dennis noticed. "Did I stick my foot in it again? Did I make you uncomfortable?"

"No, your foot is fine just where it is. It's been awhile since I've received that kind of attention. I like it though, don't let me stop you."

Dennis leaned forward—I thought for sure he was going in for a kiss—but instead he pulled his wallet out of his back pocket. "Why don't I pay the bill and we can be on our way."

I let him pay the bill and told him I'd meet him out front after I ducked into the ladies' room. Once there, I sprayed some mouthwash into my garlic dungeon of a mouth—just in case a goodnight kiss was in my immediate future—fixed my hair that didn't need fixing, and joined the Sergeant for the walk back to his car.

• • • • •

Dennis called me the next night and we had a great post-Pasta Bella conversation, and he also brought up my brother again.

"I've been thinking about what you said about not getting very much support from your brother and I was curious about something. Before your dad started showing signs of dementia—and by the way, I'd like to meet him—was Jonathan as unpleasant, cruel, and despicable as he is now?"

I cringed. "I don't remember saying he was despicable, but I know what you're saying. You see, Jonathan has always played the older brother card with me but without all the dripping sarcasm and harshness of his current dementia-aversion personality. Did I tell you? My sister and I tried to talk Jonathan into attending an Alzheimer's support meeting but he shot down that suggestion right away. I mean you'd think—"

"Did you suggest he go to the same meeting you attend?"

"Yes, and no. I did, but I also suggested other meetings and he dismissed those as well because, as he put it, he didn't need a crutch."

"Obviously he does need a crutch, but you can't make him realize that. Most people have to come to terms with their need before they'll seek the salve for it."

"God, you're good. It's no wonder Sean improves under your care and Frank considers you the Second Coming of Christ."

Dennis huffed into the phone. "Hardly, to the latter at least. I just hope you get the family help you need, and that someday your brother starts taking on some responsibility."

"Thanks for that, me too." Then I let out a very loud yawn before I could squelch it.

"Sounds like I've kept you up past your bedtime."

"I'm tired, that's for sure, but it's not your fault. The longer the days get, the more difficult it is for me to fall asleep. I love the daylight and all, but my body gets confused and doesn't know when it's supposed to shut down for the day."

"Well, I'll let you go. Thanks again for last night, can't wait to see you tomorrow."

"Me too. Bye-eee."

We hung up. Bye-eee? What am I, sixteen years old?

TWENTY

All I ever wanted growing up was to have a relationship where my brother respected me as an individual, and for the most part he did. Now, however, I wanted him to stop breaking down our dad and join my quest to build him up. I considered the wisdom in Dennis's ongoing musings about my brother. In the near future, however, my sister would be coming to Seattle to visit us so rather than have an immediate discussion with Jonathan to unearth the motivation for his mean-spirited persona, I opted to wait until her visit. I'm not a serial procrastinator but I'm also no dummy when dealing with someone who may take exception to what I have to say. I thought it best to wait for the time when the Colleen/Patty/Melanie team is assembled in one room with the offending party.

In the meantime, the Medic Alert® thingy arrived in the mail the previous month so Dad's now sporting quite the coveted look with his double-banded wrist. I mentioned it to the support group at May's meeting and they seemed to think the same thing we did: it's a good stop-gap measure before my family has to make some tough decisions regarding Dad's well-being.

Mom used to always say that you didn't have to look far to find someone in worse shape than you. Even three years after her passing, she knew what she was talking about. Sometimes the caregiver updates at my support meetings were rather innocuous—at least comparatively so for those dealing with dementia—but that was not the case at yesterday's meeting.

Eddie's fifty-seven-year-old wife, Katherine, overdosed on her daily medications a couple weeks ago. He came home from work to surprise her for lunch and she was passed out on the couch in her own vomit. A quick glance at the kitchen countertop showed Eddie what he needed to know: a full week's worth of pills were scattered on the counter minus those that Katherine managed to ingest. The doctors pumped her stomach in the Emergency Room but kept her overnight for observation. Katherine insisted she didn't try to off herself—her words—that she just got confused and doubled up on her morning medications.

Eddie's lesson, and our lesson as a result, was that Katherine could no longer read the medication instructions he'd posted on the cabinet door above her pill case. To paraphrase his words, "I used bright pink poster board and wrote super large letters in heavy black marker pen thinking that the bigger I wrote, the easier it would be for her to follow the directions." Obviously that was not the case for Katherine and may very well portend the future for the rest of us who still let our loved ones manage their own medications.

Ugh.

Victoria's husband wandered away from their house during the night without her knowing. George had been gone for at least an hour by the time she woke up and discovered his absence. She found him two miles away, still in his pajamas, barefoot, and scratched up from stumbling through other people's yards and walking through blackberry bushes. That was the last straw for Victoria; she decided to find long-term care housing for George. At her advanced age as the primary caregiver for her husband, that sounded like a good decision on her part.

Going by the standard that bad things happen in threes, Frank Campos's story was the next one on the docket. Actually, Dennis told the story to the group members because he was with Sean when it happened. While caring for Sean at Frank's house one day, Dennis went outside to do some yard work so Frank wouldn't have to tackle it on the weekend. Sean said he preferred to stay inside, so Dennis left him watching Seinfeld reruns, Sean's favorite show.

A half-hour later, Dennis returned to the house to refill his water bottle and spotted Sean crouched in the fetal position on the floor and shaking uncontrollably. It turned out Sean had inadvertently changed the channel to CNN and caught a story about a recent aerial attack on Syria that was quite graphic in its content. To hear Dennis explain it, Sean experienced a pretty severe post-traumatic reaction. Thank God Dennis was there to help and was wise enough to know that Sean needed medical attention.

After calling Frank at Boeing, Dennis took Sean to the Veterans Hospital where Sean's dad joined them an hour later. The ER doctor prescribed a sedative to be taken for a few days but didn't feel a stay at the hospital was warranted. Dennis camped out on Frank's couch that night just to make sure Sean was over the worst of it. That was the day Dad was supposed to meet Dennis for the first time but we rescheduled for the following Monday.

That Monday Dennis and I spent a fantastic evening with my dad. Dennis was so courteous, and admirably long-suffering of Dad's silly humor. As a matter of fact, Dad told the same joke three times in one hour and Dennis laughed every time; my heart skipped a beat just witnessing that. And my dad? So cute, he entertained Dennis with family stories, including the one about how he and Mom met. I'd almost forgotten that one.

Dad's first employment in sales was as a shoe salesman at Nordstrom. Mom was working in a manufacturing plant and was on her feet eight hours a day so she wore out her bargain-basement shoes fairly rapidly. After saving up her money, she decided to purchase a respectable pair so Nordstrom was where she went to get them.

When Mom walked into the women's shoe section Dad and another guy raced to get to her first; the other guy lost. Dad claims it was love at first sight—of her feet. As he put it, "She had the most delicate feet I'd ever seen."

I guess as a shoe salesman, you get to see some pretty raunchy looking extremities so when he saw Mom's perfectly manicured toes and her petite-sized five feet, he decided right then and there that he never wanted to let them go. And as the saying goes, "The rest is history."

Yes indeed, it was a great introductory dinner for my dad and Dennis. Dad told me later that he thought Dennis was a great guy but hoped he would stick around for a while. He still struggled with the concept that the Sergeant was retired military and wouldn't be returning to active duty, but Dennis and I figured the more Dad saw him, the clearer would be the understanding that Dennis was here to stay, and that was a good thing.

• • • • •

Today's Senior Center dance with the support group and their family members is the second chance for my dad to spend time with Dennis. Mike, the support group facilitator, volunteered as Disc Jockey for the afternoon. Knowing the age spectrum represented within the group, Mike put together a variety of songs in his iTunes library that were sure to get our feet moving. The one family member not present at the dance was William, but Mike, Frank, Dennis, and Eddie assured Mary that she would have many partners from which to choose for her dancing pleasure. George appeared in fine form, his move into the dementia care unit at a North Seattle assisted living facility a week away. Victoria was in heaven enjoying the opportunity to act as though everything was normal, even though the exact opposite was true.

I made it clear to anyone who would listen that my dancing skills were a bit rusty but I was willing to join today's dance extravaganza even if it meant making a complete fool of myself. I wasn't convinced Mike's first announcement would make much of a difference in that respect.

"It's my pleasure to introduce Leanna Green, our dance instructor for this event. Leanna is a retired ballroom dancer who teaches numerous types of dance throughout the Puget Sound region. Additionally, she volunteers her time to teach classes at senior centers, just like our very own Midtown Senior Center. Leanna, take it away!"

Our instructor started by running the group through some easy warm-up exercises and then looked to Mike to officially get things started. "Victoria told me that George enjoys Cab Calloway music so we're going to start with the song *Jumpin Jive*. Tell me Leanna, do you think you can offer some moves that might fit the song?"

"Totally!"

No sooner had the instructor walked us through some very basic Jitterbug steps, than George pulled Victoria to the center of the gym floor and led his wife into a jive dance—modified for their age and bodily limitations of course—drawing instant applause from the group. Dennis whispered, "Who would have thought it possible to remember dance steps from so long ago? That's awesome."

Mike slowed down the music a bit and Leanna taught a few refresher waltz and foxtrot steps as the group took turns pairing up and dancing to a Josh Groban tune. Kelly and Donna seemed to be in their element, enjoying the opportunity to break from their normal routine and spend time with the support group members and their loved ones. Rose was glad her husband was able to take a long lunch break so she and Gabe could enjoy the experience together. Sean and Rose's sister, Sophia, paired up, not seeming to mind that their dance steps didn't come close to resembling those of the dance instructor's.

Mike's next announcement took everyone by surprise. "Leanna agreed to teach the group a fun dance that is celebrated each year in honor of the performer, Michael Jackson. You all may—or may not—be *thrilled* to know that she's going to teach you a dance called *Thriller*. The dance itself is very involved, but Leanna will teach us a couple of the steps and we'll repeat those steps for the duration of the song."

Although not everyone was familiar with the music or the artist, everyone did surprisingly well learning this quintessential MJ dance routine. Speaking for myself, the fact that Leanna dumbed-it-down helped only marginally.

What a sight we all were. Sean and Sophia didn't quite execute the moves as instructed, but seemed to have fun nonetheless, Dennis and I laughed through our efforts as we endeavored to move Michael Jackson-style through the so-called easy steps, and to everyone's total delight, Dad paired up with Mary and although they didn't fare as well as some of us—which wasn't saying much—they thoroughly took advantage of the opportunity to let loose and not worry about the outcome. That seemed to be the trend followed by most.

After a lemonade break Mike slowed down the music a bit with Paul Anka's song, *Put your head on my shoulder*, a blast from the distant past, but the version being sung today was by Michael Buble.

I had no problem getting Dennis to dance with me. "Dennis, I'm having so much fun today. I haven't danced since, well, I haven't danced in quite some time. I'd forgotten how much fun it can be."

"Fun for some, but not for everyone, I'm having a hard time keeping up with you."

I stopped dead in my tracks and took his hand. "I'm sorry, I wasn't thinking. Would you like to sit down and rest a bit?"

Dennis cracked up when he realized that I thought his "handicap" was what caused his lameness on the dance floor. "Did you think my bum leg was making me dance this way?"

"I don't know, you said you were having a hard time keeping up."

Dennis pulled me to his chest and gave me a quick kiss on the cheek. "I'm afraid that would be the case even if I had two good legs. I enjoy dancing, I'm just not very good at it."

"Okay, as long as you're sure."

Then Dad interrupted us. "May I please have this dance?"

Up to that point, he didn't seem very interested in the prospect of shuffling across the floor, but since dancing a tune with Mary, Dad appeared to have warmed up a bit. Earlier in the afternoon, he had spent a good portion of his time with George. The two men swapped disjointed pieces of stories, distracting George enough that he ignored George Two in the room's wall-length mirror.

Dad and I took the traditional waltz stance. I looked him in the eyes. "Are you having fun today? Are you glad I convinced you to join me?"

"Why of course I am sweetie. I told your Mom last night that today would be the first time I'd danced since she and I were newlyweds. I think she was happy that I decided to get out of the house and kick up my heels a wee bit."

"I really like this group of people, they're a good addition to my life."

"I bet ya' like that Dennis fella too."

"Yes, Dennis too. I still miss Allan, but I think he would approve of my boyfriend, don't you?"

"Why of course he would." Then Dad asked, "What does my granddaughter think of him?"

I stopped dancing. "Yelena? Patty's daughter?"

Dad had a bewildered look on his face, not looking at all convinced that's what he meant. "Oh, that's right, you and Allan didn't have any children . . . or did you?"

I resumed dancing and tried to steer the conversation onto more comfortable ground for both of us. "No, we never got around to it."

I looked over Dad's shoulder at Dennis who gave me a little wave. "Are you sad I didn't give you any grandchildren?"

"Sweetheart, there's still plenty of time for that."

I again stopped dancing, looked Dad in the eyes and said, "Trust me, that ship sailed a long time ago."

What he said next had me laughing so hard, I gave up trying to finish the dance.

"Oh, is that boyfriend of yours in the Navy?"

TWENTY-ONE

After we went to Mass and visited Mom the previous weekend, Dad expressed his desire to go to confession sooner rather than later, so I arranged to take him Wednesday before the mid-week five o'clock Mass. The way he expressed his desire was to say, "I owe the church a confession." Catholics around the world understand the feeling of obligation—followed by guilt—regarding many things related to their religion. As a young family, we of course had the weekly Mass obligation, but also Holy days of obligation, the Easter marathon called the Triduum, and of course confessing our sins whether or not we were even aware of them.

I opted out of tonight's confession and left Dad in a pew with the others who were sitting and waiting for their chance to confess face to face with a priest out in the open at the top of the altar. I didn't want to be a discourteous bystander watching these devout Catholics doing something they strongly believed in so I hoped it wasn't sacrilegious of me to check my e-mails while sitting at the back of the church.

I looked up from my phone when I heard the distinctive clearing of Dad's throat that signified he was about to say something important. I saw him sitting earnestly and respectfully face-to-face with the priest, one of the saddest scenes I had recently laid my eyes on. My wonderfully innocent father, and in my eyes pure specimen of a human being, felt he had enough to confess that he would put himself through this ritual in front of—well—God and everyone.

I guess I just don't buy it. What I don't buy is that somehow or another my dad felt guilty and sinful; a good man who was and is forthright, giving, and even somewhat naïve in many respects. I was not a fan of this ritual but would never share my well-developed cynical thoughts on the church's practices with Dad. I respect his lifetime of following the traditions of his natal church. What is important about today's ritual is that he feel cleansed and more prepared for his afterlife. I can get behind any practice that provides my dad with that degree of emotional and spiritual comfort.

His confession lasted a mere five minutes. I hope the priest didn't make him feel guilty for whatever my dad laid on the table for the priest to forgive. I tested the waters by approaching the subject as soon as we got in the car. "How do you feel? Was this a good confession as far as confessions go?"

He smiled broadly. "Yes, this was a very good thing that you allowed me to do. I appreciate that you left work early to make it possible for me. I feel so . . . fresh, and renewed."

"If you ever want to go again, just let me know, okay? I'd be happy to take you as often as you want."

"That's very nice of you, sweetie." Dad tapped me on the hand and added, "You know, since you were already there, it wouldn't have hurt for you to cleanse your soul's palate as well."

"Not needed Dad. If I didn't feel I could talk to the Man Upstairs without a human intermediary, I'd have been damned long before now. I'm good."

We ended our field trip by going to the Blue Star Café for a bowl of that clam chowder Dad had raved about a while ago but I never got around to ordering. Boy was he correct in saying it was good chowder. One bowl, plus a couple hefty slices of warm buttered bread, put me in a food coma so when I returned to my condo, I was ready to call it a day, and so I did after a good night chat with the Sergeant.

TWENTY-TWO

"Hi kiddo, great timing. I was just about to go on a jog, now I don't have to."

"Don't let me stop you, I'll call you back in an hour or so." I felt quite proud of myself for putting Pilar on edge.

"No, seriously, I don't mind cancelling my jog, unless you want to finish working on that knitting project with the buttonholes that I helped you with a while ago." I guess two could play at this game.

I just laughed because I hadn't done a darn thing on that sweater since I tricked Pilar into making most of the buttonholes for me. "All right, you win. I think we both know each other too well to get away with trying not to do something we know we should be doing."

"Sounds confusing . . . what's new?"

"I can't remember if I told you that with my sister-in-law's help, I lined up the get-together to confront my brother about how he treats me and my dad. Oh, and since my sister is also in town—she's staying with Dad tonight—Patty will be at the head-to-head meeting as well."

"Hon, you gotta remind me of what's on your agenda. I know your boyfriend encouraged you to more or less give Jonathan the benefit of the doubt until you could discover the source of his off-putting behavior, but I need more to go on to discern what y'all have in mind. And by the way, before we end this call we're gonna set a date for me to come to Seattle so I can meet your guy, you got that?"

"Agreed. I guess the goal of the meeting is to try and unearth the source of my brother's rudeness, but more than that, Dennis opened my mind to consider that I'm not the only one struggling with Dad's dementia."

"Yeah, but Jonathan doesn't even have that much contact with your dad, how big of a struggle can it be for him?"

"I don't know, but I think I have to focus on what might be

causing him to not want to be involved. I mean, come on, Jonathan used to be a decent guy and he and I never had this kind of disconnect prior to this whole Alzheimer's fiasco."

"Why do you think now is the right time to confront him rather than months ago, or even months from now?"

That was a good question, a question for which I think I had the answer. "Believe it or not, I miss my brother, and I get the feeling Dad misses him too."

I plopped down on the loveseat; Ramona joined me and with a lick and a huff, laid her body across my outstretched legs.

"Let me tell you a story. There was a time when I was jealous of Jonathan and Dad's relationship. Dad was pretty old-school so he never considered grooming his daughters to go into real estate with him. But Jonathan became our dad's weekend realtor-in-training as soon as he turned thirteen years old. You see, on the weekends, Jonathan spent one-on-one time with him, going to open houses and spending time with Dad at the office. Patty couldn't care less about all that, but I guess being the baby of the family, I felt left out, which to me equated to being loved less."

"You poor thing. Seems hard to imagine considering how close you are to your Dad now."

"I know, but that close relationship with Dad didn't come until years later. So way back when I was a self-centered pre-teen, I let my jealousy and anger break through the surface, acting kind of like the way Jonathan acts now."

"I can't imagine that at all."

"Oh, I was not a happy camper. I refused to talk to my dad, or Jonathan, and when Dad reached out to me to have a father/daughter activity, I shunned him. God, I was so stupid, I rejected the very thing I craved—his attention."

"You little brat."

"Don't I know it? That's the kind of "ah-ha" moment I had coming out of my discussion with Dennis. I could be way off track, but I think it's worth pursuing."

"Be sure to call me after your family meeting. I need assurance that you're still alive after the confrontation."

"Don't forget, it'll be three women against one guy. Maybe

Jonathan's the one who needs to worry."

"Good point. Okay, now, about coming to Seattle to meet your boyfriend, October is wide open for me so pick a weekend, any weekend, and I'll be there."

We settled on a tentative date a couple months from now and under pressure from Pilar, I texted her a couple additional photos of the Sergeant. She responded to my text faster than ever before. "Gotta ask again, does he have a twin brother?"

TWENTY-THREE

It was great having my older sister in town. As is always the case, when Patty walked into my condo the whole place lit up, including Ramona who loves her Aunt Patty. No doubt my doggie will choose the warmth of Patty's bed over mine the next two nights, and I'm okay with that; at least we're keeping it in the family. Speaking of family, Patty and I strategized on how tonight's dinner with Jonathan and Melanie should pan out. We decided to wait until we've each had a glass of courage before we launch into our interrogation and try our utmost not to gang up on him, even though all three of us—including my sister-in-law—want to wring his neck.

Melanie is such a fine hostess and even though she and Patty had seen each other *maybe* six or seven times in the span of twenty years, they carried on as though they were besties—if that friendship designation is even applicable to people in their fifties. One drink later, Patty and Melanie retreated to the kitchen to work on the brie and brioche. I was stuck with Jonathan, so acting more confident than I felt, I dove into that night's hidden agenda.

I sat on the loveseat next to his recliner and caught him before he flipped on the television. "Jonathan, I need to ask you something."

"What's stopping you?"

I wanted to say my entire fifty years of history with him and the fear of him bullying me into submission, but I opted to say, "I want to get along better with you, I'd even settle for how we used to be as kids when you teased me to no end. It feels like any semblance of civility stopped about the same time Dad's senior moments began."

"What's your question? You said you needed to ask me something."

Hardass. It was a mistake having this conversation without the sisterhood that was conveniently hiding in the kitchen. Those bitches,

I'd deal with them later. "Here's my question: who are you? Here's another: why are you so mean to me and intolerant of Dad?"

I stood up—I was on a roll and needed better traction. "You criticize what I do for him and you make fun of him when his dementia symptoms dare to rear their ugly head in your presence."

I paced the living room. "You act like Dad has control over his Alzheimer's. Do you think he enjoys the experience of gradually losing the parts of his brain that he's relied on his entire life?"

"It's difficult to watch."

"Well, how do you think *he* feels? Imagine how embarrassing it is for him, asking the same question over and over again. Or . . . or when he forgets the names of his grandchildren, or whether he even has grandchildren."

Colleen took a calming breath. "I know it frustrates him and although he's never specifically said so, I'm sure he's scared to death—how could he not be?" I returned to my seat and noticed the sisterhood being very quiet in their protective foxhole.

In the next moment I didn't realize Jonathan was talking until I looked directly at him; he barely spoke above a whisper. "Growing up, everyone said I was the spitting image of Dad: my looks, my mannerisms, even my jokes."

I'd forgotten that my brother used to be quite the crack-up.

"When I became a realtor, no one was surprised. 'He's a chip off the old block' was the common sentiment. When I became a real estate broker, many people warned me that I had big shoes to fill after all of Dad's success."

"Right, you've done real well for yourself. Aren't you proud of what you've accomplished? I know Dad is."

"Yes, I'm proud, and I've always liked the fact that I have a career that mirrors his. Hell, I used to look up to him—"

"Are you saying you don't look up to him anymore? He's still the same man who raised us. Deep in his core he's still our dad, the disease hasn't changed that."

"Easy for you to say."

I couldn't believe he'd said that. "Actually, not really."

My brother got to his feet. When he turned towards the kitchen I saw from his expression that Patty and Melanie must have joined us in the room. "Everything has changed, but not in the way you may think. Like I said, I grew up being just like Dad, and up until he started to go all geezery on us, I didn't mind."

Geezery? I hated when Jonathan used derogatory terms but I let that one slide.

"I used to want to be just like him, but now I'm afraid I will be." Jonathan stood in place, crying like I'd never seen before; literally, I've never seen my brother cry.

I beat Melanie to the punch and put my arms around him and while he continued to cry, I said, "It's not a sure thing that just because Dad has Alzheimer's you, or Patty and I for that matter, will get it too. I can't focus on that right now and you shouldn't either. I'd rather focus on who he is and try to enjoy every moment we have with him."

Melanie spoke up, having moved next to her husband to put her arm around his waist. "She's right, Jon. If you continue to be paralyzed by your fear of the disease, you'll miss out—and so will I—on the life that we can have with your dad in spite of the disease."

Jonathan managed a smile and said, "You've been watching *way* too much Dr. Phil."

I was grateful for that interjection of humor. The rest of the evening was far from perfect. Time may heal all wounds but we were all sporting some pretty fresh ones. Jonathan made it excruciatingly clear there would be no overnight transformation on his part, meaning he still wasn't going to help out in any substantive way. I guess denial can be quite the stubborn monster. If you don't acknowledge the problem, it doesn't exist, or if it does exist, it might go away if avoided long enough.

If only that were true.

• • • • •

For the remainder of Patty's visit Jonathan didn't have any opportunities to practice what we'd preached at him. My sister met Dennis on Saturday when he took us out to lunch in Pioneer Square. He introduced us to an Italian restaurant I had yet to frequent: Il Terrazzo Carmine. I deemed the restaurant a solid contender with Pasta Bella, and my sister deemed Dennis an exquisite choice on my part. What can I say, my sister and I have good taste. Patty and I spent Saturday evening with our dad and cooked one of his favorite meals—not lasagna this time, rather, corned beef and hash, the Quinn family way.

On Sunday, Mom had an extra visitor at Calvary Cemetery. After Dad and I talked to her for a while, filling her in on the latest and not so greatest news since the previous week, Patty lingered at the gravesite, putting in her own two cents. Must have been more than two cents, however, because Dad and I waited on the bench near our car for a good twenty minutes. For the past couple years, my visits have been a great time to clear any air I felt needed clearing where my mom was concerned, and being here made me feel like I was in her presence. Patty, on the other hand, had visited Mom's grave just one other time, and that was the day Mom was buried. I guess Patty had some air to clear as well.

TWENTY-FOUR

Those of us in the wedding industry rely on summer weddings as our most profitable time of the year, and that's the case for *Brides by Sarah* as well. For several months now, I've struggled to stay focused at work, and wondered if my store and staff management duties were up to par. Sarah cleared that up for me when we had breakfast at Macrina Bakery before opening the store today.

"First of all, I want to say that I admire all that you do for your dad. It can't be easy balancing work, trying to have a social life, and always being 'on' where your father is concerned." My boss took longer than necessary to take another sip of her latté.

"I think I hear a 'but' coming."

Sarah put down her cup. "The truth is, I've noticed how distracted you've been. You check your cell phone for calls or texts numerous times throughout the work day, you've lost some of the vibrancy you used to exhibit toward our clients, and you rush out of the shop within seconds of finishing your shift."

"I'm sorry, I can stay longer if you need me to—"

"That's not necessary. I spend more time at the store than you because I own the place, I don't expect you, or any of the staff, to work beyond your scheduled shifts."

Sarah shifted in her seat. "I don't think I handled that well . . . my reason for talking to you is that I'm worried about you. For the most part, your work hasn't suffered, it's just that I'm concerned that you're doing too much in general."

That comment caught me off guard and made me defensive. "Well, there's lots to do. My sister lives in California, my brother is no help whatsoever, and my dad requires more and more of my time. Add to that, I'm trying to fit in a romantic relationship that I enjoy a whole bunch, but I'm not getting enough 'me' time."

"I hear ya' there. Even the great stuff in our lives—significant others included—require time and attention to where even going on a date becomes just another item on the multi-numbered *To Do List*. Am I right?"

"Yes, but I don't want to lose this guy—he's good to me and for me. Dad likes him too, you should see the two of them together."

"Hold on there. Do you honestly think your boyfriend would walk away if you spent less time with him, especially if that time was spent having restorative time for yourself? That doesn't sound like someone you'd pick to be in a relationship with."

"It doesn't, does it?"

I reached across the café table and put my hand over Sarah's. "You're right. I've been so caught up in finally having a social life I'm worried I'll do something to jeopardize it, even though I believe without a shadow of a doubt that Dennis would understand and give me the space I need." I squeezed her hand and then placed my hands on either side of my face. "Argggh! I'm way overthinking this whole thing. The next time I talk to Dennis, I'll let him know how I feel, and tell him what I need. I'll just get it over with, rip off the Band-Aid, jump into the deep end."

"I wouldn't go that far, but it sounds as though you get the idea. I'm not here to tell you to change anything about your life that you don't want to change, but I *am* here to tell you that I want you to take care of yourself. If that means you need extra time off or want to shorten your work shifts, that's okay too."

Sarah picked up her purse. "Look, it'll be the fall season pretty soon and as usual, business will start to slow down. If you'd like to work less hours from fall through year-end, that would be fine with me. Perhaps making that work adjustment will smooth out the more pressing stuff in your life. Will you think about it?"

That evening I did think about it and decided that twenty to thirty hours a week would be manageable finance-wise—if I made an effort to pinch my pennies—and very manageable time commitment-wise. I hadn't planned on dipping into the settlement monies from Allan's wrongful death lawsuit unless I was faced with an emergency, but I guess this situation qualifies as such—there was no hope of Dad getting any better so his need for me would only increase. Having more time to balance the goings-on in my life could definitely work towards everyone's advantage and would be a wise use of my rainy day fund.

TWENTY-FIVE

The greatest benefit of working less hours was being able to spend more fun-time with my father. Each week in September we did touristy things that he hadn't been involved in for many years. His energy level and walking abilities continued to decline, but our abbreviated participation was well worth the effort.

After Labor Day, when the tourists had gone back to their respective states and most schools were back in session, our first adventure found us at the Woodland Park Zoo. The very kind employee who sold us our tickets asked if we were interested in renting a wheelchair or an electric cart for Dad, an offer he proudly turned down after looking behind him for the intended recipient of said offer. I knew we could see more of the zoo if he used a cart, but I chose to honor Dad's wishes to visit on his own power rather than see more of the zoo and have him feel embarrassed riding in what he labeled a Senior Citizen mobile. As it was, we were able to tour the Northern trail with its brown bear, Arctic fox, elk and wolf exhibits, and on our way back to the entrance of the zoo, Dad was quite taken with the snow leopard attraction.

We had a lunch snack while sitting on a bench in the zoo's North Meadow where we relished the opportunity to watch young and old alike ride the vintage carousel, an installation at the zoo since 2006. Dad shocked me by talking about the significance of the carousel, providing facts that I would have assumed were previously lost in the plaques and tangles now residing in his eighty-five-year-old brain. I was thrilled to learn that the carousel was built in 1918, all of the forty-eight horses onboard were hand-carved in wood, and this carousel was one of only one hundred fifty wooden carousels remaining of the five thousand that were originally built starting in the early 1900s.

I knew without a doubt that everything Dad said was one hundred percent accurate, and because I knew that, I was saddened that the most recent memories—including details about his own grandchildren—didn't make it out of his brain's plaques and tangles, those nasty brain invaders that arbitrarily preserved and killed vital parts of his brain.

• • • • •

Towards the end of September, the partially-inside Seattle Aquarium was my attraction of choice due in part to the very seasonal rain the area was enduring but also because Dennis had not yet visited this waterfront amusement. I felt obligated to invite him so that I could again strip him of another Seattle-area virgin item.

As soon as I arrived at the Aquarium I had to visit the little girls' room so I left my father with Dennis and suggested he might introduce Dad to the boys' facilities should he need to partake. He did. Unfortunately, I took longer than the men and once I rejoined them, Dad was beside himself with worry.

"Where did you go? This young man and I were worried sick you'd gotten misplaced somewhere."

I looked at Dennis who shook his head, which I knew meant he hadn't worried, but my dad had. "I'm sorry I took so long . . . I guess my vanity got the best of me so I took the time to brush my silver locks, not wanting to embarrass my two handsome men in public."

Dad retained his frantic look, not at all appeased by my explanation. To be honest, he looked a bit peeved, so much so I wasn't convinced our tour would even get off the ground. Then Dennis effectively intervened, as only he could.

"It can be frightening when we're in an unfamiliar place with mostly unfamiliar people, isn't that right Mr. Quinn?"

Dad looked from Dennis to me then back to Dennis, and seemed to calm down a bit. "I agree with you young man, it's dark, and somewhat off-putting down here." Then Dad took off his glasses, wiped them, and said, "I'm sorry, what was your name again?"

Dennis reintroduced himself and Dad reciprocated by letting the

Sergeant know that he could call him Patrick.

We took an abbreviated tour, mostly checking out the *Window on Washington Waters* and the *Underwater Marine Mammal* viewing center—both of which totally captured my dad's attention. He, like most of those who visited the latter, found himself enchanted by the antics of the sea otters. Each time they performed for us captivated humans, Dad laughed as though it was the first time he had seen them, even though most of their tricks were repeated over and over during the twenty minutes we lingered at the exhibit. I hugged Dennis's waist and took in the sight of Dad's joyfully childish response to the underwater animals and took a mental snapshot of the sight to be revisited in the months ahead. I took a cell phone snapshot as well.

After all that excitement, Dennis and I noticed that my dad looked pretty tired so we ended the tour and headed to the car. Today's outing convinced me that my days of going solo on most car outings with Dad were coming to an end. The visuospatial aspects of his dementia severely messed with his ability to maneuver from the pavement to the inside of the vehicle. I guess he lacked the dexterity and know-how to accomplish the task. I felt so sorry for him—he literally shook with fear when we tried to help him release his foot off the pavement to place it inside the floor of Dennis's SUV. I know for certain that I would never have managed without Dennis's strength and assistance.

After we settled Dad in the back seat and shut the door, I whispered to Dennis, "Thank goodness you were here to help. It's getting to the point where I can hardly manage his weight without potentially hurting both Dad *and* me."

Dennis kissed me lightly on the cheek and before opening the front passenger door, said, "You don't have to. I'm yours whenever you need or want me."

I felt inclined to take him up on both of those offers.

TWENTY-SIX

Pilar's visit to Seattle was upon us. I didn't know who was more excited because both of us desperately needed a best friend fix. Not only was my friend anxious to meet Dennis, she was also interested in seeing my dad as it had been a year since she was last in Seattle.

I saved Dennis for the second day of her visit. That left Saturday afternoon open for some quality dad-time after Pilar scoured a few Seattle area yarn stores for new inventory items for *Peace, Love, and Yarn*. She made it to my condo by four o'clock, parked her 1960s Volkswagen Bug in one of the two visitors' parking spots for my building, dumped her backpack and bags of yarn in my guest room, and then we drove over to Dad's for dinner.

One of the many things I love about Pilar is her excitement for life paired with her unconditional love for people; okay, that's two things, but they always accompany her wherever she goes. That exuberance blew into my dad's house as she bowled past me to grab him in a bear hug. "Patrick you ol' coot, look at you, you don't look a day over eighty-five."

Uh oh, Dad had no idea who this whirling dervish was and why it was whirling in his house.

"Dad, you haven't seen my best buddy, Pilar, in some time. You probably don't recognize her because she's gotten very decrepit looking in her old age."

Pilar shoved my shoulder in a combination, I-think-you're-just-kidding-but-if-you're-not-I'll-deal-with-you-later maneuver. "Your daughter's right, I've been hiding out on the island for so long I've lost all ability to behave appropriately in public. I'm the friend who saved your daughter from wallowing in sorrow and despair time and time again throughout her elder years. Without me, she'd be a shadow of her former self."

Pilar did a quick head-nod in a "take that!" effort at getting back at me.

Dad took off his glasses, wiped the grime off them, and looked through them again. "Why didn't you say so? I know you, you're that hippy friend that my daughter's always talking about who has some sort of mongrel that her own dog plays with."

Pilar looked at me, placed her hands on her hips and said, "Mongrel?"

I assured Dad that I would never talk about Pilar's dog, Tristan, in that manner and that he must have her Chesapeake Bay retriever confused with some other Chesapeake Bay retriever that I've known in a past life. With that given explanation, I asked Dad if he wanted to watch the Seahawks game while my hippy friend and I threw together the grub for the evening. He thought that was a great idea which was a good thing because I needed to mollify Pilar by explaining that Dad oftentimes comes up with not so appropriate statements when he's confused or under pressure. Thanks to almost two decades of friendship, Pilar accepted my explanation.

· · · · ·

She filled a pasta pot with water and whispered, "Your dad kind of looks like he did a year ago but he has a vacant look in his eyes, like he's not totally engaged in the action. Is that normal?"

"It is now. I think part of it is that he can't follow conversations as easily as he used to. It's as though his brain is on a treadmill that can't keep up . . . like it stumbles and loses its footing. For example, right now, he's watching the football game but there's no way he can follow the intricate plays. He hones in on some of what the announcers say and every once and awhile can follow the scoreboard, but he misses out on most of what's going on."

I broke up the ground beef in the fry pan and added the onions to prepare for the bottled pasta sauce.

Pilar pulled me towards her and gave me a hug. "For the past year or so, I listened to all the stories you told me and I understood the gist of how difficult it was for you and your dad, but nothing compares to seeing him in person to get a sense of what the disease has taken away from him. I'm so sorry Colleen."

Another thing about Pilar and her exuberance is that whether she's happy or sad, she exhibits an equal amount of the stuff. For instance, right then she was bawling and wouldn't let me go—that's when Dad joined us in the kitchen.

"Colleen, is there something you need to tell me? Are you trying to get out of the closet?" Dad looked at each of us, back and forth, back and forth, and then my best friend and I cracked up. Pilar left the room to blow her nose and compose herself. I stayed put to tell Dad that I wasn't trying to get out of the closet, but if I ever did he would be the first to know, and then I lied and told him that Pilar had a severe reaction to the onion I just cut and she needed to hug it out. I waited to see if my shading of the truth had worked and when I saw that it had, I asked him to keep us company while we rustled up the rest of the meal.

Yep, Dad was okay with that explanation and the one about the closet when I reminded him that I have a boyfriend. I wasn't at all certain he remembered Dennis, but he seemed to remember spending time with a male friend of mine not too long ago . . . like yesterday.

•　•　•　•　•

I was jealous of Dad's total acceptance of a new sweater Pilar knitted for him and gifted him with after dinner. I mean come on, I've rarely seen him wear the vest I made him several years ago, but as soon as Pilar helped him on with the sweater, Dad gave serious thought to never taking it off; I'm not certain he did. I saw him the next day to visit Mom and he was wearing the same clothes with the same pasta sauce-stained khakis topped with his new favorite wardrobe item: Pilar's custom-designed zip-up cardigan with a dark green Celtic cabling pattern, the latter a nod to my dad's Irish roots.

After our visit to the cemetery I got Dad settled at home—to return for dinner later—and I met Pilar at The Five Spot on Queen Anne for brunch with the Sergeant. Dennis beat me there so by the time I arrived, Pilar and my boyfriend were as thick as thieves in one of the highly sought after booths, yacking it up as though they'd known each other for as long as . . . well, as long as Pilar and I have known each other. Some women might feel threatened by the instant connection between her boyfriend and another woman; not me. The fact that Pilar found camaraderie from the get-go, and Dennis was instantly at ease in my best friend's company, made me extremely happy.

Much later, after brunch, after Pilar had returned to Whidbey on the four o'clock ferry, after Dennis and I ate a light dinner with my dad, and after Dennis left my place around ten in the evening, Pilar and I connected by phone to compare notes from our weekend. We both agreed that from now on Pilar was in charge of knitting clothes for Dad, and she decided if she was to have any more quality time with him, she needed to make more frequent visits to Seattle. Pilar also concluded that she had no qualms about my continuing to develop a relationship with the Sergeant because he met her two requirements for me: he was mighty fine and I was the happiest I had been in many, many years.

Pilar wanted to know why Dennis made me so happy, and I told her. "It wouldn't be fair to Dennis, or any guy I happened to date, to compare him to Allan. I think when you compare one person to another, you've already done both of them a disservice. Allan was a unique person, with a unique personality and an admirable strength of character. Dennis matches that same profile but in his own way.

"What is fair to talk about, however, is that one of the differences of dating in one's 50s or 60s is that at our age we've lived through a lot in our adult years, whereas when Allan and I got together in our 30s, we hadn't been true adults for very long. Dennis and I bring a lot of life experience to the relationship which can be good and bad, I guess. Given what Dennis and I have experienced in our past, however, we've managed to glean helpful lessens from the ups and downs in our lives. We seem to have moved on from the not-so-great times because we turned those into teaching-times. And here's something that stands out where Dennis is concerned—what you see is what you get, and although he's not super communicative, what he has to say when he does talk is well-worth the listen."

"Can you imagine if he was a chatterbox like you—or for that matter, like me? The competition to get one's point across would be pretty stiff."

"That's the truth, and yes, Dennis is a very good listener. You know, I might tell him something—even something as mundane as what goes on at work—and weeks may pass when all of a sudden he'll bring up that episode as it relates to something we're currently talking about. When he does that, it always catches me by surprise, and quite frankly, it's flattering. Again, it shows that he listens and that he cares about what's going on in my life."

"It must be so nice to have someone tuned-in to you like that."

"It is."

"That reminds me of something I read a while ago, but shoot, I can't remember where I read it . . . anyway, I memorized it because it said precisely what I was feeling at the time: 'It can be very isolating to think there's no one who cares when you get a paper cut.' Wow, it makes me just as sad now as it did when I first read it. I'm a basket case I guess."

"That's where you're wrong, I care if you get a paper cut, just like you've cared about everything that's happened to me throughout our friendship. You'll always have me and I'll always have you. Nothing changes that."

"We're lucky that way, aren't we?"

"Yes, we are."

After I hung up the phone I had to think about that luck angle for a while. I didn't know if luck and hope were inter-related but it would be good if they were. I do quite well in the hope department—I don't find it at all difficult to hope the best for everyone in my life—but I'm not convinced that having hope is enough to get the job done this time.

I hope I'm wrong.

TWENTY-SEVEN

Ten months ago, Dad's and my lives changed forever when we received his Alzheimer's diagnosis. Now here we were, same place, different year, to go over the results of a new series of neurological tests Dr. Nesbitt ordered to determine any patterns of change since the last time he saw us. He's also going to go over Dad's current medication regimen. I was taken aback by Dad's request to meet with Dr. Nesbitt alone prior to the three of us sitting down to discuss the tests' outcomes, but I sat in the waiting room while he and the doctor spent a good twenty minutes together without me.

I didn't recognize any of the desperate-looking family members and their fading loved ones this time around; no doubt this was a new batch of afflicted ones, a scene most likely duplicated each day in this doctor's waiting room. I was so distracted, the nurse had to call my name twice before I heard her. I felt okay when I first arrived, but I wasn't certain that would be the case when I left.

I entered the doctor's personal office. "Hey, Dad, long time no see!"

Dad gave a literal retort to what should have been a comical greeting. "Sweetie, it hasn't been a long time, I just saw you a few minutes ago. Are you feeling a wee bit dim today?"

I apologized for trying to lighten the mood, took my assigned place at the conference table, and set up my tablet and pen. Looking at Dr. Nesbitt I said, "What's up Doc?" Then he told me.

"Before I give you my impressions of your father's latest testing, I want to fill you in on Patrick's and my conversation just now."

I looked at Dad who refused to make eye contact with me. "What's going on?"

"Your father told me he's not comfortable living by himself. Even with the safety measures put in place by the family, he feels very ill at ease when he's alone—both day and night. He doesn't feel at all comfortable taking walks, so he's not visited with his friends for quite some time."

I couldn't believe what I was hearing; if what the doctor said was true, Dad had been less than honest with me when he recounted stories from his war buddies' coffee klatch. I turned to him. "Is this true?"

He lifted up his head and although he didn't look at me, once he started talking, there was no stopping him. "I'm so sorry, Colleen, I should have told you sooner but I'm afraid to be alone. I used to be able to talk to your mother but that doesn't work anymore because I get the feeling she's not listening to me. When I used to talk to her, I felt like someone else was in the house with me, and that was nice. Now I don't even have *that* to fill my day."

Then my dad looked directly at me. "Also, you want me to call you twice a day but each time I do, it takes me longer to figure out how to do it."

I had noticed Dad's calls were getting more and more past the assigned morning and evening times.

There was more.

"I don't heat up the meals sufficiently that you and Melanie make for me, so most nights I eat them partially frozen."

I slapped my hands over my mouth, closed my eyes, and then the tears started falling as Dad continued.

"I don't hardly clean myself because for some reason the shower water isn't comfortable on me anymore. And I don't always make it to the bathroom on time because I keep misplacing it—the bathroom. One time I walked into a very small room and almost started to take a leak before I realized it was the closet. That time I didn't make it in time."

I held up both of my hands. "Dad, stop, please stop." I cleaned up my face with the tissues the doctor had passed to me, turned my chair to face my dad, and scooted my chair closer to him. "I'm sorry you're not comfortable living alone in your house. If I had known how you felt—better yet, if I had noticed all these things you're now telling me—I would have figured out how to make things better for you."

I turned to Dr. Nesbitt, "How come I didn't know about all these issues with my dad? I see him at least four times a week, how can I be so dense?"

"Don't beat yourself up. Your father is similar to many of my patients who either come from a highly functional social or work environment and/or are inclined to have a well-tuned sense of humor. I know it doesn't sound as though the two go together, but they do. Your father's neurocognitive deficits juxtaposed to adequate verbal fluency and excellent social comportment and poise might tend to disguise his neurocognitive limitations in many settings."

Dad looked me straight in the eyes. "What did this joker just say?"

If I didn't know any better, I would just laugh it off and move on. Mind you, I didn't understand everything the doctor said either—at least not in the manner in which he said it—but what I understood him to say was that without intentionally doing so Dad was able to hide many of the dementia symptoms he had been experiencing. I felt a little bit less guilty about my lack of awareness, but not much.

"Dad, if you'd like, I'll move into the house so you won't be alone. There's plenty of room for you, me and Ramona. What do you say, you wanna be roomies?"

My dad had no difficulty coming up with an immediate answer. "No. I love you Colleen, but I don't want to live with you."

Dr. Nesbitt exited the office under the guise of needing to make a phone call; no doubt the doctor figured Dad's and my conversation should be a private one.

"You have a life, Colleen. You can't be with me every minute of the day and night, and I can't imagine either of us would enjoy that."

"Okay, how about hiring someone full-time to live in your house who can do what needs to be done to make you more comfortable living there?"

"No, I don't want a stranger living in your mother's and my house. I'd rather live someplace new, but a place where I don't have to worry about anything other than getting up in the morning, having a place to eat and pee—without mixing the two up—and being with other people so I have company when I want to have company."

I had the feeling he was talking about some sort of assisted living place and Dr. Nesbitt confirmed that assumption when he returned to the discussion.

"Patrick and Colleen, I put together some resources for you to review together that should help you decide what type of senior housing scenario feels right for you." He handed Dad the packet. "You'll see that I put bright orange sticky notes at locations that also offer memory care assistance. I think you would be wise to start there."

I looked at Dad and saw him smile for the first time that day, a smile perhaps fueled by the comfort of knowing that very soon he would be able to relax and leave many of his cares behind. If he felt better, then I'd do my best to feel better too. "Okay Dad, after the doctor finishes up the rest of this appointment, we'll head on out and see what we can do to find you a new place to live."

The doctor's assessment more or less mirrored what Dad had described earlier in the appointment. He was losing his ability to be independent one step at a time, and the fear that change in condition brought about caused Dad to lose the greater portion of his quality of life.

• • • • •

I took Dad home. While he went to the little boy's room, I made tea preparations. While I waited for the water to heat up, I took a look around the house and saw things I hadn't seen before—the house looked uncomfortable, not lived in. Whereas before, it seemed as though Dad's presence filled every room of the house, now the occupied areas were reduced to one corner of the living room and his bedroom. It looked as though he was uncomfortable with more space than that.

Dad joined me in the kitchen. "Phew, that feels better. Some people get a load off by sitting down and putting up their feet—for me it's emptying my bladder."

"I heated a pot of water for tea, do you want a cup?"

Dad sat at the kitchen table. "That's just what the doctor ordered."

I placed both our mugs on the table. "How about a snack with your tea?"

"Tea's fine. Why don't you sit down?"

I did and immediately started to cry. Dad pulled a couple paper napkins from the plastic holder on the table and handed them to me. "Are you not feeling well Colleen?"

I guess that's an appropriate question for him to ask; I didn't feel at all well but it had nothing to do with my health. I bunched up the paper napkins, blew my nose, and took a sip of tea, all the while gathering my thoughts.

"Oh, Dad, I feel like such a dunce, and I feel so guilty as a result."

"Now, now, no need to be so hard on yourself . . . I heard that somewhere lately, where was that?"

"Dr. Nesbitt."

"Oh yes, the Doc, well, no need to spill any tears over me. I'm an adult. I don't expect you to babysit me for pity's sake. My talking to the doctor wasn't meant to make you feel bad."

"But I do feel bad, I—"

"No. I never intended for you to spend your adult life looking after me. When your mother was alive, we both agreed we wouldn't place our kids in that role. We made plans to never let that happen and budgeted our finances accordingly. Me wanting to move out of this house isn't a reflection on you, it's me feeling lost and at loose ends on my own."

"Won't you reconsider and let me move in with you?"

Dad patted my hand and shook his head. "I love you but I don't think living together is the answer to my brain problems."

"But like I said, we could hire someone—a male companion even—to keep you company so you don't feel lost anymore."

Again he shook his head. "This house is a family home. Once some medical person moves in here, all of its charm will disappear. I won't let that happen."

I took both of Dad's hands in mine. "I seem to be making this all about me and I apologize. I just wish there was something I could do."

"There is. Find me a new home."

TWENTY-EIGHT

Two weeks after Dad's painful neurological confession, Jonathan actually offered to accompany Dad and me on our search for appropriate long-term care housing. Truth be told, I kind of cringed when my brother stepped in to help. I guess I was being stubbornly proud to maintain the misguided belief that I didn't need anyone's assistance in all matters regarding Dad. I capitulated to his involvement, however, figuring that my brother's real estate experience—combined with my passionate advocacy—would best serve the task at hand. At the close of our first day of touring facilities—after much online research on both Jonathan's and my parts—we concluded that this hunt would take longer than a day, so Jonathan cleared his calendar for the week.

We pulled up to the fifth assisted living facility that week and girded our loins for what was to come. We weren't fully enamored with the previous four facilities but we put Dad's name on a waiting list for the dementia care units of two of them. My brother and I suspected that this venture wouldn't be a walk in the park but we were shocked at how high the demand was for a facility that offered dementia care.

High demand wasn't the only part of the search that was shocking—the monthly fees made us feel as though we were looking for an upper Eastside Manhattan loft rather than a facility for adults needing some tender loving care. Dad wasn't the least bit concerned, however. He told us that he and Mom saved mightily for a rainy day, and according to him he was well-prepared financially, regardless of the size of the downpour.

"Dad, this is the last place in the geographical area that we all prefer. The outside looks pretty nice but man, there's a lot of traffic on this street. Don't you think it'll be kinda noisy?"

Of course Jonathan had an answer for that. "Hey kid, that's the least of our concerns. I think most of the folks moving into geezer places like this don't have the best hearing to begin with." With a smug expression he added, "And it's not as though there's much demand for a mountain or ocean view at this stage of their lives."

As we walked into the lobby, I elbowed Jonathan surreptitiously and gave him the Colleen Strand evil eye and whispered, "Utshay upway, adday isway otnay away eezergay e'shay away eniorsay itizencay." My pig Latin was lost on him but at least it prevented him from repeating the g-word again. "Come on, let's go inside and meet with the marketing person. What's this one's name?"

Jonathan checked his notes. "This time we're meeting with a woman named Polly Mitchell. There's her office on the left." Jonathan knocked on the outside of the doorframe to get her attention and Ms. Mitchell got up from her desk to greet us.

"You must be the Quinn family." Jonathan introduced us, and she asked us to call her Polly and led us into her well-appointed office.

"It's very nice to meet the three of you. Let's sit down and have a visit before we take a tour. Can I get you a beverage?"

Dad reached out his hand to Polly, "My name is Patrick, what's your name?"

Polly shook his hand and after introducing herself personally, she added, "Will you be the family member moving into Seattle Gardens should you decide this place is to your liking?"

Dad's fine-tuned humor was in excellent form. "Well Polly, if I had my druthers, my son here would be one of your newest residents, but seeing as I'm the one who might fit better into this fine establishment, I guess I'll go in place of him."

After that comment, I figured maybe we'd just let Dad take over from there on out, but first I had a concern that needed addressing. "We need to know if you have a waiting list for this building. We've already put Dad's name on two lists so I want to get that concern out of the way."

"That's a very appropriate question to ask. Seattle Gardens just went through a major remodel when another senior housing company purchased the complex. Initially, the new owners stated their plans to expand the general assisted living area but the seller insisted that if the sale was to go through, the new addition had to take place in our memory care unit. I believe you indicated, Colleen, that Patrick might be interested in that part of our community?"

"Correct."

"Okay Patrick, I'll explain what we've done here. Prior to the sale of this community almost nine months ago, the memory care unit, called The Gazebo, consisted of eight studio apartments of varying sizes. When the remodel was completed a month ago, that increased to fifteen studios. Some of the apartments had to be reduced in size to accommodate the additional units, but it's a nice tradeoff being able to have more availability. Before the remodel, we had five people on the waiting list. That list cleared as of this past weekend, so we have two apartments still available."

Dad sat up to his full sitting height. "Can we take that tour now? I don't want to waste yours or our time talking until we've seen what you have to offer. When I've seen the place I'll know if it's right for me. If it is, then we can talk details."

We toured the assisted living areas first, and then Polly approached the secured memory care unit. "We have this security panel both on the lobby side of the main portion of the building and on the other side of the door. You'll see the hint panel that contains four rows with large and small numbers on each row. That particular detail isn't important to review right now, so why don't we go and have us a visit."

With a surreptitious push of a few buttons on the lobby side panel, Polly opened the door and welcomed us to the memory care section of the facility.

After viewing the two available studio apartments and the activity and dining rooms, Dad told us he wanted to rest a bit. "You three youngsters go have a chat if you like, I want to meet some of my new friends here in what you call The Gazebo."

I looked at him and tried to discern if I understood the gist of what he just said, then he clarified it for me. "For the record, I want the apartment at the end of the hallway. Whatever number that is, that's the one for me."

Jonathan cleared his throat and admonished Dad. "Look, you don't even know how much it costs. I think you're making an ill-advised, knee jerk decision. Let's go home, sit down, look at the bottom line, sleep on it, and then decide what's best for you."

"Sorry Son, I beat ya' to it. I have a pretty good idea of how much money I have, I know what I want, and I want that apartment at the end of the hallway."

Ms. Mitchell then addressed Dad, "It sounds like you've found a new home with us. Welcome home Mr. Quinn."

I turned to Ms. Mitchell, "Well Polly, you heard my dad, I guess we're done here. Let's sit down in your office and do what we gotta do to get the ball rolling while my dad gets to know his new neighbors."

Oh my word, Jonathan was beside himself. He was ready to wear his big boy realtor pants and negotiate a deal he could live with, but that's not how it's done—at least not when the veteran realtor, our dad, already knew what he wanted. When we sat down to handle the business-end of the tour, Jonathan complained about the small size of the studios for the price being charged. I squelched that complaint by pointing out that the relative small size of the studios was a non-issue because of the other common areas available to the residents.

I did have one concern however. I told Polly that Dad liked to walk around a lot so the staff might have their hands full. "What you've mentioned is more the norm than the exception. If a resident is mobile, their room isn't a place where they spend the greater portion of their day. We encourage each resident to participate in the social and activity programs here."

I was glad Polly mentioned the fun part of living here. "So what would Dad be doing? What types of activities do you offer?"

"If it's okay with you, I'd like to invite the Health & Wellness Director to this meeting. If she's available she'd be the best person to fill you in on the programs we offer to assure our Gazebo residents a great quality of life. I think you'll be impressed."

Forty-five minutes later, we finalized Dad's reservation for an apartment. I told Polly that I would come back the next day to provide the financial information and sign the pertinent paperwork needed for automatic billing purposes. Because of the way I was usurping my brother's feigned authority, Ms. Mitchell correctly concluded that I would be the main point of contact for both the financial and health aspects of Dad's residency.

Feeling duly dismissed, Jonathan left to retrieve our dad—having been told the combination for the secure keypad—and I set up an appointment with the Health and Wellness Director so that Dad could be assessed to determine his health and cognitive needs. If all the ducks cooperated and lined up in a row, he could very well move to Seattle Gardens, and his end of the hallway Gazebo apartment, by Thanksgiving.

•   •   •   •   •

Dad passed his facility assessment with flying colors but that didn't mean everything was hunky dory on that front. I admit I was somewhat oblivious—not in denial, just oblivious—about the severity of his Alzheimer's disease progress. We already established that Dad would no longer be responsible for taking his own medications, which is a good thing. Someone at the facility would provide him with his supplements and medications, which included an additional Alzheimer's drug called memantine. It's a well-known fact that Alzheimer's drugs don't work if you don't take them, nor do drugs for prostate issues.

In addition to medication assistance, Paula Tremaine, the Health & Wellness Director at The Gazebo, detailed the type of assistance Dad would need with his Activities of Daily Living, or ADLs.

• Personal hygiene: bathing, grooming and oral care.

Dad always looked dapper in my eyes, I mean we live in Seattle for God's sake, anything goes is the guideline that applies to clothing and grooming. I conceded, however, that he may need assistance with the bathing aspect if showers made him uncomfortable.

• Dressing: the ability to make appropriate clothing decisions and physically dress oneself.

He had this one in the bag. My intention was to make sure all his clothes remained clean and in good shape so I volunteered to take charge of the clothing maintenance duties so Dad didn't have to pay extra for someone else to do it.

- Eating: the ability to feed oneself, though not necessarily to prepare food.

No problem there, Dad seemed to enjoy the concept of eating and now that he'd receive hot meals—instead of Melanie's and my frozen ones—he'd do even better. Dad wouldn't be charged for eating assistance at this time.

- Maintaining continence: both the mental and physical ability to use a restroom.

I was pretty sure the mishaps he had at home would become a thing of the past—at least I hoped he wouldn't relieve himself in other than the appropriate location; that would be problematic.

- Transferring: able to move oneself from seated to standing and get in and out of bed.

Granted, this last ADL can sometimes be a challenge. Paula said the staff would monitor Dad upon his arrival to discern if any assistance was needed—something I was on board with because I sure didn't want him to be stuck in bed or in a chair just because his coordination wasn't as keen as it used to be.

But those are just the basics. He will need cuing to do all of the above innocuous activities and cuing comes in the form of a helpful paid staff person. In other words, not cheap. Dad said he had the finances covered and I discovered he wasn't exaggerating. Sure, he turned over his day-to-day finances to me months ago, but he had yet to advise me of the fact that he purchased some valuable stocks way back when.

I had to wonder where I was when my parents were buying Microsoft, Apple, and Amazon stock. I mean it, where was I? Apple stock was first offered in 1980 at $22 a share, Microsoft in 1986 at $28 a share, and Amazon in 1997 at $18 a share. I was in my mid-twenties in the eighties, was twenty-something dollars totally out of my network? And come on, there was no way I couldn't afford $18 a share for a few shares of Amazon in my mid to late thirties. I'm ashamed at my lack of vision, but thrilled with that of my parents.

I guess time will tell as to how long Dad's fortune will last while living at Seattle Gardens. He was bowled over by the place so the formula I live by is that when Dad is happy, I'm ecstatic. But the reality of the situation is that at move-in, Dad's monthly rent and care fees will total just under $6,000. Even if his care fees never increase—highly unlikely—that's still just under $72,000 a year. What percentage of people have that kind of money?

My brother took on the task of selling our parent's fully paid-off house so that sale will provide a healthy windfall to Dad's piggy bank. I was in charge of helping Dad determine what he wanted to bring to his end-of-the-hallway apartment, what to keep for us siblings, and what to sell or donate. Fun and games to be sure, but both Patty and Pilar agreed to schedule a trip to Seattle the week before, and including, Thanksgiving day, so the burden would be equally spread amongst us gals.

I again counted my blessings that I downsized my work schedule until the end of the year. Even with some extra hours of "free" time each week, this chore promised to be a daunting one.

TWENTY-NINE

One year ago I was in crisis mode having just learned of dad's Alzheimer's diagnosis; that crisis brought me to my first Alzheimer's caregiver support group meeting. For this year's December meeting, I was coming out of a comparatively manageable crisis, but one of the other regulars had just climbed out of a Defcon Level 5 catastrophe. Going back to my Mom's premise that you didn't have to look far to find someone worse off than you, Eddie stood up to the plate.

"Katherine and I pulled into our driveway after a long workday—me from closing up my auto repair shop and Katherine from helping out on one of our son's landscaping crews. As soon as I put the car in park, Katherine was out the passenger door, running towards our elderly neighbor, Gloria, who had just picked up her mail. Seeing my wife approaching, Gloria put out her arms to her—we've been friends of Gloria's for years so it's not unusual for lots of hugs to be exchanged. Katherine wasn't looking for a hug. She stood in front of our neighbor with her hands on her hips and accused Gloria of being a thief.

"Of course Gloria had no idea what Katherine was talking about and feeling threatened, looked to see if I was close by. Katherine then yelled at Gloria and accused her of stealing a turquoise scarf when she was at our house for dinner the previous night. I walked up to them and asked what was going on. Holy crap, Katherine started poking Gloria in the chest and with each poke she enunciated each word, saying, 'This lady took my scarf and I want it back!' I pulled Katherine away from our neighbor—Gloria is eighty-two years old for God's sake—and told Katherine to go into the house. Boy did that get her going. She dropped a few f-bombs—a pretty common occurrence as of late—and stormed into the house.

"By that time our neighbor was so shaken up I had to help her into her house and onto a chair in her front room. I was sure she was gonna have a heart attack or stroke-out on me, it was that bad. This sweet neighbor of ours promised she didn't take Katherine's scarf, and asked if my wife was okay. Hell no, she wasn't okay, but right then I was more concerned about Gloria than anything having to do with my wife. I got Gloria a glass of water and handed her the telephone because she wanted to call her son to come over and sit with her for a while."

Victoria said, "My goodness Eddie, that's just horrible, is everything all right now?"

Eddie rubbed his forehead. "No, everything's not all right, not even close. Long story short, Gloria's son did go to his mother's house and then stormed over to ours. He explained that although he understood the difficulties we were going through, he made it very clear that what happened that evening must never happen again. I pleaded with him to be patient with us, reminded him that this was the first time something of this nature had happened, and that I would bring Katherine to her doctor for a check-up."

Frank turned to Eddie. "What did the doctor say?"

Eddie looked at Frank and shook his head. "There's more. After dinner that night, I thought Katherine had calmed down—I mean she seemed interested in a television show she was watching so I went out to the garage to change the oil in my truck. I wanted a break from my wife and leaning over an engine seemed like a good way to do that. Unfortunately, that break didn't last very long. Whether it was the disease or Katherine herself that became violent, one or the other stormed into the garage while I was looking under the truck's hood. Apparently she grabbed the first thing she saw—a five quart bottle of engine oil that was on the garage shop counter—and threw it at the back of my head, slamming my body into the engine compartment and then to the ground, knocking me out."

I couldn't believe what Eddie was telling us; it sounded more like an episode of *Cops* than a real life experience of one of my caregiver friends. Eddie then summarized the rest of that episode by telling us details that he learned after he had regained consciousness in a hospital emergency room.

Seeing what she'd done, Eddie's wife ran next door to her

neighbor's house for help. Brian, Gloria's son, had opted to spend the night with his mother so when he answered the pounding at the front door and saw Katherine, he was good and ready to defend his mother and himself. After hearing Katherine's frantic explanation about Eddie's garage accident, he grabbed his cellphone, dialed 911, and followed Katherine back to the house. As one of the paramedics loaded Eddie into the ambulance, Brian filled in the other First Responder about what transpired earlier in the evening, implying that it was possible Eddie's accident may have been instigated by his wife. Katherine was allowed to join her husband in the ambulance with the intention that everything would be sorted out in the emergency room.

Once Eddie was conscious, he explained his wife's condition to the ER staff and the Seattle police officer that had been assigned to investigate the incident. Eddie admitted that this latest incident could have only resulted from her actions, which then triggered his wife's 72-hour hospitalization on Harborview Medical Center's psychiatric floor, and Eddie's overnight stay in a general patient room to be monitored for a concussion.

Eddie was discharged the next day but his wife was not. Eddie figured that with all the ramping up of Katherine's aggressive behavior, a three day mental health assessment was a good idea. He also admitted, a bit reluctantly, that he needed some time away from his wife, which all of us agreed was a good idea. When he brought Katherine home, she promised Eddie she would be good from now on and begged him not to lock her up and throw away the key.

Whoa.

When it was my time to share, I barely talked about Dad's move into Seattle Gardens, other than to say that he was so happy to be out of his house he could be found cavorting around his new home as though he was the staff social director. No one at the meeting believed the cavorting report except Dennis who had seen my dad in action the past three weeks.

I told the group that I went back to my full-time work schedule earlier than originally planned and Dennis supplemented my facility visits by spending time with my dad there. In the past few weeks, he and Dad worked on a Battle of the Bulge jigsaw puzzle that had the residents and staff members oooing and aahhing over their accomplishment. Dennis also got down and dirty with Dad when Dad insisted on pulling weeds in The Gazebo garden—even though they had died in the cold weather. Also, the three of us spent a good portion of every Sunday just hanging out. Most days, when my dad slipped into his room for a nap, Dennis and I spent time getting to know the staff and a few of the residents.

Frank told the group—I already knew of course from my and Dennis's conversations—that his son Sean was now attending the Veteran's day program several days a week. He attributed his son's ability to do so to the successful work that Dennis—my boyfriend!—did with Sean the past year or so. Did that mean Dennis would no longer attend the caregiver meeting in the future? That's up to him, but I had plans to keep him a part of my life so not seeing him at the meeting was no biggie for me.

Victoria had some fun news to share. She started out by reminding us that when George first moved into his assisted living place five months earlier, she didn't like visiting him at all because the other people in the memory care section were further gone than him. She felt she was looking into a crystal ball and seeing her husband's dreary future. The past two months, however, she volunteered at the facility by holding the weekly story time for any residents who could sit still long enough to listen.

"George still doesn't know who I am, but for some reason that no one at the facility can understand, when he and the residents are told that story time is going to take place that day, George stands in the hallway facing the memory unit's entrance door waiting for me to arrive. One day I was running late and one of the staff members noticed George was tiring a bit so they brought over a chair for him to sit in—and sit he did, still looking earnestly at the door for my arrival."

I asked if her husband still sat next to her when she read. "Oh yes, he's so attentive and he still puts his arm around my shoulders. And he always looks right at me, doesn't look anywhere else but at me. Even though he doesn't know me from Adam or Eve, there's something there, I'm convinced of it."

I told her I was certain he still had a viable connection with her and the rest of the group agreed.

The facilitator ended the meeting early so we could have a mini Holiday celebration for the remaining twenty minutes. What followed was a bit of socializing, and a considerable amount of commiserating, as we said our goodbyes until the first meeting after the New Year. Dennis and I took our leave to attend another gathering, Seattle Garden's Holiday extravaganza. Would the action never cease?

THIRTY

With Dad no longer living in the family home, another of my New Year's Eve traditions fell by the wayside. My very astute boyfriend told Frank about my dilemma and they put together a new tradition—New Year's Eve at the Frank and Sean Campos compound. I was excited to spring Dad from The Gazebo and with December 31st occurring on a Sunday this year I felt as though I was doing something to honor Mom by taking him on an outing.

Within two weeks of moving into Seattle Gardens our Sunday visits with Mom at Calvary Cemetery came to an end. That event signified two things for me: Dad completely lost interest in attending Sunday Mass, and he stopped making mention of Mom. Whatever the reason, he had moved on, now fully engaged in his new life at his new home.

When we arrived to pick Dad up for the party, the residents were just finishing their early afternoon snack. I had dined two or three times a week with Dad since he moved to The Gazebo, and Dennis came with me a few times to enjoy the fine cuisine, but what I saw in the dining room this time absolutely floored me: my dignified, respectable father sitting at a table wearing a bib. I purposefully walked behind him and unsnapped the offending clothing addition.

"Now how did this thing get here? Someone must have mistaken you for someone else." I then walked into the kitchen to talk to the attending caregiver.

"I don't want my dad wearing a bib, he's not a child, he's a full-grown man and I won't have him degraded by being adorned with a baby accessory." I guess I'm the only one who took exception to the bib because the caregiver calmly explained that all residents wore a bib once it became too difficult for them to coordinate the eating process. I looked towards the dining room and witnessed what she was talking about. My dad's shirt already had a sploop of applesauce on the front of it. I apologized, telling her this was a first for me and it would take some getting used to.

When Dennis took Dad into his bedroom to change his shirt I had a come-to-Jesus moment with myself about overreacting and taking it out on the caregiver; the way I came off when I reprimanded her was totally out of character for me. Later that evening Dennis equated my actions to those of Marshawn Lynch—former Seattle Seahawks football running back—known for his 'Beast Mode' way of playing. I accepted the Sergeant's gentle reprimand and made a note to think before acting the next time I felt beastly.

. . . . .

The Campos party was a blast. Dad and Frank's son were quite the pair. Sean was by no means normal in the traditional sense of the word, but he was a true gentleman and acted very deferential to his fellow soldier, my dad. What really impressed me, however, was how Dad and Sean seemed to supplement each other's deficits. Sean filled a plate with food for Dad and helped him sit at the dining table, even helping him with the eating process; Dad acknowledged Sean's word processing difficulties but let the younger man take as long as he needed to construct sentences out of those words.

After a thoroughly delicious feast Dennis and I cleared the plates and Frank and Sean stayed in the kitchen to make the final dessert preparations. Back in the dining room, Dennis and I returned to our seats across the table from my dad, and held hands under the table. Dad turned his attention to Dennis.

"You remind me of my son-in-law Allan, Colleen's husband." Then turning to me, "Sweetie, where is that husband of yours? Wasn't he invited to tonight's dinner?"

Whoa, this was new, I didn't know what to say that wouldn't alarm Dad or hurt his feelings. If I reminded him that Allan died almost eight years ago, he might get sad. If I told him that Allan stayed home tonight, he would wonder why I was two-timing my husband by being here with a date. In the span of five seconds I recalled a word Mike had used at a recent meeting: redirect. "Dad, hasn't this been a fun evening at Frank's? Looks like we have a new tradition to bring in the New Year from now on."

That clumsy sleight of hand on my part—though not exactly brilliant—detoured Dad's line of thought. He easily adjusted to a new topic and said it was nice to meet new people and added that he didn't miss our New Year's dinners at the place where he used to live. Frank and Sean returned to the dining room and ten minutes after all of us admitted not having room for another bite of food, the five of us had a sizable slice of pumpkin pie with varying amounts of whipped cream piled on top.

We didn't think Dad had it in him to stay awake for the televised East Coast New Year's Eve celebration, so Dennis and I drove him home to The Gazebo and left him in the very capable hands of his favorite caregiver, Virgilio. Dennis and I weren't interested in any additional celebrations other than our own, so we called it a night and headed to my condo.

THIRTY-ONE

January and February were busy months at the store. With summer brides ordering their gowns and their bridesmaids' dresses, we hit the ground running. The good news was that compared to last year, going back to forty hours a week was a doable schedule now that Dad was in the capable hands of The Gazebo staff. At the most recent support meeting Victoria encouraged me, saying that I could now enjoy being just a daughter instead of first and foremost a caregiver. She had that same experience when her husband became a resident of his long-term care facility; she was able to be his wife instead of being the person on whom George depended for everything. Life was good, but still not the status quo that I'd been craving for several years now.

When I called to talk to Pilar one day in March, I asked her if I was being selfish, wishing for a long season of status quo. "Are you kidding me? Come on girl, everyone needs and likes a few periods of monotony in their life. I take great comfort in the same-o same-o and have learned to enjoy it, knowing it will be short-lived. But back to you, what does status quo mean to you?"

I rubbed Ramona's neck as she nuzzled close to me on the couch. I gave some thought to Pilar's question.

"I don't know, I guess it means nothing new happening in relation to my dad's Alzheimer's, and Jonathan finally doing something to help me."

"Hold on a minute, Jonathan helping you is anything but status quo."

"You're right. Truthfully? I don't want Dad to get any worse because when he gets worse it means he's getting closer to leaving me."

"Damn, I'm so sorry. Has there been any change regarding where he is on that scale thing that measures his cognitive decline?"

Pilar nailed it on the head. The reason why status quo doesn't exist anymore is because Alzheimer's had proven to be an aggressive moving target. Gone are the early days of looking at the GDS scale and celebrating that Dad was between a three and a four out of seven. The most recent measurement of his decline had him between a five and a six.

"That's right, I didn't tell you the latest. Dad is now considered to be in the moderate to moderately severe level of dementia. That puts him about a step and a half away from the maximum on the scale."

"You're gonna have to give me details, what is it about your dad's current status that puts him there?"

I pulled out the Global Deterioration Scale brochure that Dad and I looked at more than a year ago and told Pilar the symptoms currently applicable to my dad. "Listen to this laundry list of symptoms, and I quote: 'can no longer get by without assistance with his ADLs; unable to recall major relevant aspects of his life or even extremely recent experiences in his life; disoriented as to date, day of the week or season; doesn't require assistance going to the bathroom or feeding himself.'"

Pilar latched onto the last thing I mentioned. "Well, that's a good thing. So if or when he does need potty help, would that be the triggering behavior that would push him closer to the seven on the scale?"

"Unfortunately, a seven on the scale entails far more than that. Here's what's in our future, and again I quote: 'may occasionally forget name of spouse' I guess in our case, it would be may occasionally forget name of daughter."

Pilar encouraged me to read further.

"Here goes: 'may be incontinent of urine and/or bowels, verbal abilities will be lost, need for feeding assistance' and here's the biggie, 'lose the ability to walk.' And guess what that means?"

Pilar didn't answer.

"I'll tell you what that means according to my computer research. It means his muscles will atrophy, he can get pneumonia because of the cessation of physical activity, and in the final stages, he'll lose the ability to swallow, his organs will shut down . . . you get the picture."

Pilar's crying was the only sound on the other end of the line. I felt sudden remorse. "Oh my God, I just ruined your day. Was that TMI? Talk to me, Pilar."

"I hate Alzheimer's. I hate it more than I hate jogging."

"You hate jogging?"

"Of course I hate jogging, I only do it to make you happy."

"I'm sorry, you don't have to jog anymore."

"Thank God, but I still hate Alzheimer's. I don't want Patrick to reach seven on that goddamn GDS scale."

"I never wanted him to be a one, but that's what the cards dealt—"

"Well it's a lousy goddamn hand. Demand a new one."

I told Pilar that I had already asked the Universe for a reshuffle, a redo, and an about-face, and the Universe just stuck its tongue out at me. The Universe did the same to Eddie's wife Katherine when she welcomed a perfect stranger into the house while Eddie was out in the garage. The stranger was a magazine salesperson and managed to convince Katherine that she needed a half dozen or so subscriptions. Fortunately Eddie came into the house right as Katherine was searching for a credit card and he promptly escorted the stranger out of the house and demanded he never return.

The Universe also did a number on Rose's sister Sophia. She had a massive stroke and now lives in a nursing home that costs $15,000 a month. The 'bright' side about that situation was that the two sisters' finances were separated so Sophia qualified for Medicaid.

I then told Pilar that just like all the nasty diseases out there, Alzheimer's is no respecter of persons. You can be a loving, tender, and light-hearted eighty-six-year-old man and still get it. You can run a successful landscaping business one day—like Katherine—and turn into a gullible, trusting fifty-seven-year-old woman the next. You can be a highly respected accountant one day—like Sophia—and lose your independence the next day because progressive vascular disease first took away your reasoning abilities and then rendered your body immobile.

After I concluded my tirade, Pilar said, "I guess no one said life was fair."

"Trust me, Pilar, I don't expect life to be fair, but I could stand for it to be a heck of a lot gentler."

THIRTY-TWO

A year ago, the Sergeant and I met at Midtown Senior Center's April support group meeting. At one of my recent coffee times with Melanie, I told her that we had planned a two night stay at a cottage on Bainbridge Island the following month. Before I could ask her for a favor, she offered to be the family contact at the facility while I was away. She visits Dad once a week, which is more than I can say for my brother. Am I surprised that in four plus months, Jonathan has hardly visited our dad? Not at all. Am I disappointed? That goes without saying.

Dad no longer recognizes Melanie but my sister-in-law insists that being a friendly stranger is just as gratifying as being a familiar daughter-in-law. My dad has no idea who Jonathan is either, which is probably why my brother doesn't visit more often. It's easy for me to be extremely critical of Jonathan's logic while Dad still recognizes me, just the same, I'm confident that if my name and identity as his daughter ever escapes his memory, I'll still be faithful to him.

That trip with Dennis was a big thing for me. In the not too distant past, I didn't feel comfortable not being tethered to my dad, but that changed. I know he loves his new home—he still manages to cavort a bit, albeit more slowly—and I have total confidence in the care he receives from The Gazebo staff.

I packed that comfort in my overnight bag when Dennis, Ramona, and I took the thirty-five minute ferry ride to Bainbridge Island. We rented a dog-friendly cottage near Fay Bainbridge Park, with Ramona in mind, and a romantic view of the water, with us humans in mind.

The architect who designed this cottage knew what she or he was doing. Each window provided eye-catching views: a lush garden with early spring flowers, a soothing water feature just outside the bedroom which intrigued Ramona but was off limits to her, and a stunning view of the Puget Sound from the living room and deck. Ramona even had her own mini-room where she slept on a doggie bed at night so she didn't monopolize the bedroom's cozy queen-sized bed.

We left Ramona in her doggie room when we visited four of the seven island wineries and strolled through the Bainbridge Island Historical Museum, but we rewarded her for her patience by spending a good deal of time at Rockaway Beach Park on Blakely Harbor so she could exercise and visit with her own kind.

Dennis and I enjoyed the part about being away from everything related to our life in Seattle. Having a bit of distance from my responsibilities at the bridal salon and everything Dad, and Dennis's volunteer responsibilities at the Veterans Hospital, gave us renewed energy for whatever might await us back home.

Our island break also encouraged lots and lots of conversation about where we've been, where we are, and where we're going. We even talked about marriage as it might relate to us. Neither of us are against the idea and agreed to keep the discussion open. We realized that each of us had the same fear about marriage—that our spouse would leave us one way or another. Thankfully, that fear no longer had a hold on us.

I knew life was fragile and I'm not guaranteed the next minute— the end of Allan's life proved that. But in the years since his death— specifically since meeting Dennis—I came to realize that avoiding a romantic relationship because of that fear was ridiculous. It's interesting that Dennis totally understood my way of thinking, and I understood his. We concluded that both of us were victims of circumstances over which we had no control—I couldn't prevent the irresponsible driver from ending Allan's life, and Dennis couldn't prevent his wife from violating their marriage vows.

The possibility of marriage was definitely on the table, front and center, rather than on the back burner. If we were in our twenties or thirties, a long courtship might be the route we would take. Seeing as I'm in my fifties and Dennis just turned the big 6-0, when we think it's time to tie the knot, we'll just go ahead and do it. One thing we both agreed on was that neither of us felt incomplete as individuals. I felt that whole thing about "You complete me" was a bunch of sappy hogwash found in movies. Maybe our age has something to do with the fact that we don't rely on someone else to satisfy a checklist of must-haves in order to live a full life; instead, we look at each other as complimenting who we already are. I think when you meet the right person, the puzzle pieces fit smoothly into place so there's no need to force something where it doesn't belong.

I was fortunate to have that with my first love, and I'm doubly blessed to have it again with Dennis.

THIRTY-THREE

I left the bridal salon a few minutes after six o'clock and headed to The Gazebo for a quick visit before Dennis and I met up at the condo. It was a crazy hot June day in Seattle so I relished every opportunity to enjoy the comfort of the Seattle Garden's air conditioning before going home to my hotbox of a condo.

Dad's facility only had air conditioning in the common areas which, unfortunately, was more customary than not in long-term care. Residents could, however, use portable air conditioning units in their apartments which Dennis installed in Dad's studio the end of May and will install in my condo soon. The Gazebo staff gave each of the residents' family members a brochure that provided information on heat regulation challenges in the elderly, and what the staff would do to meet those challenges. I had no idea that the sensation of thirst decreased in the elderly so it was good to know that the caregivers would make sure Dad was sufficiently hydrated.

Once inside Seattle Gardens I signed-in at the front desk and made my way to the memory care unit. It was past the residents' dinner time so I expected to find Dad in his room or perhaps socializing with one of his friends. Instead, when I turned the corner into the common area I saw my brother sitting in the community living room in conversation with Dad. Rather than join them, I stood just out of view in an effort to give them personal time together and to shamelessly eavesdrop on what I assumed was a very rare occurrence.

I heard my brother describe one of his commercial real estate projects and Dad made appropriate comments in response to what Jonathan said. "Well sir, it sounds as though you have your hands full with that one. Do you like your job?"

Jonathan talked to Dad as a stranger would, but with utter respect. "Yes, Mr. Quinn, I like what I do, very much. You know, my father was a real estate broker many years ago. I went into the same business because of him."

"I bet your father would be mighty proud that you followed in his footsteps, I know I would be. Do you see him much? Is he aware of what you do for a living?"

I heard Jonathan clear his throat. I peeked around the corner and saw him rub his forehead back and forth. "No, Mr. Quinn, I don't see my father as often as I should, and I don't think he's at all aware of what I do for work. He's not been well and it's been difficult finding the time to visit him."

Dad rubbed his chin. "Well young man, I don't see as that's any reason to stay away from your father. If he's as sick as you say he is, he may kick the bucket before you know it. If I were you, I'd be sure to make time before it's too late."

"You've got a point there, Mr. Quinn. Thanks for the advice."

Dad struggled to get up out of his chair and Jonathan helped him. "Thank you . . . what did you say your name was?"

"Jonathan . . . my name's Jonathan."

"Before you leave, Jonathan, can you direct me to the nearest little boys' room? I have to pee something awful."

That was my cue to leave before either of them saw me. I didn't need to spend time with my dad tonight, Jonathan had that covered. I left The Gazebo and Seattle Gardens hoping that this visit by my brother was just one in a string of future visits. Like Dad said, Jonathan's father could kick the bucket at any time.

THIRTY-FOUR

As Dad often says, "Another day, another dollar." With the overtime and sales bonuses I received since January, I decided I could afford to again reduce my hours the last three months of the year and spend more time with my dad.

My belief that Alzheimer's was a moving target certainly proved true the past few months. Back in February I told Pilar that Dad was between a five and a six on the GDS Scale; since the beginning of August, he moved more towards a solid six with the start of urine incontinence. Part of that issue came about because his prostate started to act up again, but regardless of the cause, it became problematic. His doctor increased the dosage of his prostate medicine in the hopes he would experience some pain relief, and with that relief, fewer accidents. Regardless, it made sense for Dad to start using disposable adult incontinence underwear so that's now a new addition to his wardrobe.

I appreciated that the staff advised that it would be less expensive to purchase a supply of those undergarments at a warehouse store than to pay for those provided by the facility. I felt responsible for managing Dad's money—well, I *was* responsible—and with his house not selling within the first three months of being listed, Jonathan set it up as a rental to help offset The Gazebo's fees, fees that went up to $8200 a month. My how the money flies when someone has a progressive disease like Alzheimer's.

Dennis and I grabbed a quick bite to eat at a sandwich shop and then invaded the nearby Costco to purchase the needed supplies. When we located the adult diapers I was embarrassed, but not Dennis; he tossed two forty-eight packs into our cart like they weren't the pee and poop catching items they were. He was having way too much fun with this task so I changed it up a bit.

"Honey, are you sure that's the right type for you? I thought the lightweights were sufficient for your needs, not the superabsorbent."

Everyone knows you can't shop at Costco without it being as crowded as the last Saturday before Christmas. Dennis received a few pitiful looks from the women, and the men who overheard me did an about face and walked in the opposite direction; I guess they thought incontinence was contagious.

The Sergeant was a good sport, however, and he gave as good as he got. "You could be right, darling, but I've been dropping big loads lately so I think I'd better switch to the super-pooper kind." He then put his hands around his waist and shook his waistband back and forth a bit. That latest stunt cleared the aisle but he wasn't done.

"How are you on lubricant? You don't wanna run dry, ya' know."

Oh my God, now it was my turn to disappear. I was three aisles over before the Sergeant caught up with me.

When he did, we both laughed so hard we could have each used one of the undergarments we'd thrown into the cart. Dad's situation was not funny, but when you're nervous, embarrassed, or plain fit to be tied, a little bit of humor helps smooth out the speed bumps. We headed to the check-out but decided that we felt way too exposed just purchasing the incontinence products, so we put a few bottles of wine in the cart, as well as some pot stickers from the frozen food department, a two-pack of laser printer ink cartridges—one for each of us—and a bucket each of red vines and chocolate covered pretzels. That bounty made our purchase look far more pedestrian.

Even though it was after hours and Dad would be in bed, we dropped off his items so the staff would have his personal supply sooner, rather than later. Back at the condo we put away our unnecessary cart-filler items, and took Ramona for a walk. Fall in Seattle was perfect this year with a slight chill in the air and very little rain—an anomaly to be sure.

"Thanks for going with me on that errand. I don't think I would have managed half as well by myself."

"I've told you this before: when you want or need me, I'll be there for you."

I knew that, and I enjoyed the comfort that knowledge afforded me. I hugged Dennis closer and we turned back to the condo, quite certain Ramona had sufficiently checked out all the doggie smells from the past twelve hours. Dennis had an early schedule at the hospital the following day, so it was high-time we called it a night.

. . . . .

After his hospital shift the next day, Dennis went to The Gazebo with a specific agenda in mind. He arrived in time to have lunch with Patrick; afterwards they went outside and sat at one of the umbrella tables near one of the outdoor heaters. Patrick knew Dennis by sight—he didn't always remember his role in Colleen's life, but the relationship between the two men was a meaningful one.

"Mr. Quinn, I need to ask you something very important."

"Ask away young man."

Dennis turned his chair to face Patrick. "Your daughter, Colleen, is a very special woman to me."

"Well that's nice to hear. She's special to me too."

Dennis felt he needed to clarify matters. "Mr. Quinn, I love your daughter and she loves me. I confess, I love everything about her. I love her dog, her sense of humor, the way she makes me feel, the way she treats people . . . everything."

Patrick looked at Dennis with an intensity not found as of late. "I'm glad to hear that young man. I'm glad you love her and that she loves you. What are you going to do about it? Are you gonna make an honest woman of her?"

Dennis leaned back in his chair and chuckled. "Colleen is one of the most honest people I've ever met—she doesn't need any help from me—but I would like to make her my wife. Mr. Quinn, I'm officially asking you if that's okay . . . to make her my wife."

"You have my permission, one hundred percent of it. Do ya' think you might do that sooner rather than later? I'd like to be one hundred percent there, if you know what I mean."

"I do. If all things work out as I hope they will, I'm thinking two weeks from now."

"What date is that?"

"October 1st."

"Will you remind me so I don't forget? I'd hate to miss my own daughter's wedding."

"It's a deal. Thanks so much, Mr. Quinn. I'll take good care of her."

"Of course you will, but please do me a favor and call me Patrick. That Mr. Quinn stuff is getting real old."

THIRTY-FIVE

Whoa, two weeks from proposal to walking down the aisle must be an all-time record in the bridal world. Fortunately Dennis and I wanted the same type of wedding: intimate, no whistles and bells, and on the cheap. Although I steered away from any traditional bridal trappings, there were benefits to working at a bridal salon. We carried mother of the bride & groom dresses and most of them steered clear of being traditionally frumpy—Sarah always carried a few styles that a traditional mom might want to wear—but most of the store's inventory was very stylish; the latter was what I chose.

The covered courtyard of Seattle Gardens served as the venue for our October celebration. We counted on there being no rain and doable temperatures and were rewarded for our faith in the elements. We had close to 100% attendance from the caregiver group and a few of them were responsible for outfitting the occasion. Kelly and Donna gifted us with the flowers—a combination of lilacs and white orchids, Victoria provided the bride's "something old" by loaning me her mother's gray and white cameo necklace which perfectly complimented my Wedgewood blue knee-length cocktail dress, and Mike—our meeting facilitator extraordinaire—was our Officiant, a task he relished having recently been ordained a minister through an online ordination program. Jonathan and Melanie sprang for the caterer and Patty and her husband, Wade, volunteered to do all the set-up and take-down for the day—from soup to nuts as Mom would say.

Dennis and I entertained the idea of holding the ceremony and reception at Pasta Bella, our first-date venue, but thought better of it. Dad considered Seattle Gardens his new home, so we decided it was very appropriate to get married at the place where he felt most comfortable. Pilar even offered her Whidbey Island home for the occasion, but I knew that would be far too involved of an outing for Dad and most everyone else. We weren't shooting for ambiance for our nuptials; attendance by friends and loved ones was a higher priority. And I must say, without all the hoopla usually involved in a bride's wedding day, this bride was thoroughly able to focus on the people, starting with my husband-to-be. I was pleased to have a mere two weeks between proposal and wedding, the sooner the better suited my way of thinking on the matter.

My best buddy arrived from Whidbey Island two days before the ceremony to provide any help she could offer as my Maid of Honor, but mostly the two of us spent the time pretending to be twenty years younger than we were—cocktails were involved—and we enthusiastically enjoyed our girl time. Sean Campos served as Dennis's Best Man—with both of them in their military dress blues, they were quite a dashing pair. Fortunately, Dad no longer assumed Dennis would ship out and leave me high and dry, so the uniforms didn't add any undue stress to the experience. It would have been unfortunate if he thought Dennis was on the verge of leaving me so soon after getting married.

Speaking of being dressed up, Dennis helped Dad pick out a new, off-the-rack suit from Men's Warehouse—a dashing dark gray that complimented my blue for the walk down the aisle. And there we were, arm in arm, proceeding down that aisle to join the others at the front of the courtyard. With less than twenty people in attendance, Dad's and my walk was a short one, which suited his waning stamina just fine. And what some might consider a glitch, was more of an added attraction. Once he delivered me to my groom, Dad chose to stand next to me during the entire ceremony—whether out of confusion or fatherly commitment no one knew, but it didn't matter.

Dad really got into the swing of things when he chimed in with me on my "I do." He said, "We do, and that's our final answer." Somehow or other the *Who wants to be a millionaire?* script made its way through the highways and byways of Dad's brain and added a certain flair to the whole event. When Mike said, you may now kiss the bride, Dad did, followed shortly thereafter by my Sergeant in his dress blues. Yum!

• • • • •

Frank had just finished giving Colleen and Dennis hugs when he felt his cell phone buzz in his jacket pocket. He left the courtyard and walked into the lobby to answer his phone. He saw from the Caller ID that it was Eddie Turner. "Hey, Eddie, what's going on?"

"Something horrible happened to Katherine. I'm on my way now to find her!"

"Slow down. What do you mean by 'something horrible'?"

"I was showering and getting ready for the wedding and left Katherine in the living room to wait for me. Instead she left the house and walked to a bus stop around the corner and boarded a bus. God knows Katherine wouldn't fare too well on her own, and I sure don't trust strangers to treat her appropriately. There's no telling what kind of trouble she could've faced."

"Damn, I'm sorry. What can I do?"

"The police are on their way to meet up with her, and so am I. The bus driver is gonna try to keep her on the bus until I get there."

"If you need me, I'll come and help, I'm sure Colleen and Dennis would understand."

"No, I don't want them to know what's happened. I just wanted someone to know why we didn't make it to the wedding. I'm just now pulling into the bus station. I gotta go. I'll call you back."

Eddie disconnected the call before Frank could say good-bye. Dennis happened to glance towards the lobby, told Colleen he'd be right back, and joined Frank in the lobby. "I saw you on the phone, is everything okay?"

"That was Eddie. The bad news is that while Eddie was in the shower to get ready for the wedding, Katherine wandered outside and caught a bus. The good news? They're about to be reunited."

Dennis buttoned up his jacket. "Should we try to meet up with them to provide some moral support?"

"No, he was adamant that neither you nor Colleen be told about what happened . . . I guess I just blew that. He'll call me when he has something new to report."

Not wanting to draw any more attention away from the wedding celebration, Frank and Dennis returned to the reception.

• • • • •

I looked around for Dennis, having lost track of him for a few minutes while the rest of us were alternately feasting on the exceptional food prepared by Fare Start (a Seattle area job training and culinary placement program for the homeless) and dancing up a storm to the tunes that had been prepared by Mike—acting as DJ now that his officiating duties had been completed.

Back at the DJ table, Mike made an announcement. "May I have your attention? It's time for the official first dance by the bride and groom. Let's give them the opportunity to start the dance alone, and then please feel free to join them as Ray Charles sings, *Come Rain or Come Shine*.

Dennis rejoined me, held my hand, and drew me closer to him. "Are you happy with how things went today?"

"It's been fun. Dad seemed pretty with it, don't you think?"

"I'm glad he was a member of the bridal party. I asked Frank to record it for you so you'll have your Dad on video forever and a day."

"What a wonderful husband you are Mr. Dennis McGee."

"And what a beautiful wife you are Mrs. Colleen McGee."

The Sergeant moved me around the dance floor as others joined in. "Are you sure you want to change your name? I'd be totally fine if you were still Colleen Strand."

"No, I want your last name. I still have my history as being a Quinn and then a Strand—that will always be a part of who I am—but my history going forward is as a McGee. I like that."

"Thank you—for that and for enlarging my family. It's been so long since I've had family nearby. And speaking of family, it sure was generous of your brother to arrange and pay for the catering. I didn't think it would be possible on such short notice."

"I think the small crowd had something to do with that, and I agree, it was nice of my brother to handle those details."

Right then, Jonathan and Melanie danced past us; Melanie waved as she floated over the dance floor. I blew her a kiss. "Like you said before, his baby steps, although promising, will have to be enough for me until he's all-in where our dad is concerned."

Smiling, Dennis said, "Maybe it won't take as long as you think."

I leaned back. "What do you know that I should know?"

Dennis steered me away from an answer and maneuvered us towards the Best Man and my boss. "Hey, Sean and Sarah, you've got some impressive moves goin' on there. If I didn't know any better, I'd assume you took some dance lessons in your spare time."

Sean lifted Sarah's hand up in the air just as she managed to take a twirl underneath their extended arms. "No practicing needed dude. Sarah told me she's been to lots of wedding receptions and that I should just follow her lead, right Sarah?"

Sarah nodded in agreement. "You don't work in the bridal industry for fifteen years without picking up a few dance steps here and there."

After the song ended, Mike cranked up the volume, and the beat of the music, which is when Dennis and I bowed out for a bit. Rose and her husband Gabe, however, danced like it was 1999, which was timely because they were dancing to a similarly titled Prince song. Jonathan and Melanie watched from the sidelines holding hands, not feeling any pressure to cut a rug as Mary was doing with Mike. Victoria had no qualms about accepting Frank's invitation to shake her booty and they alternately danced and laughed at their feeble attempts to not make fools of themselves. Kelly and Donna danced in place, an arm around each other's waists, and rocked side to side as much as Donna's body would allow.

At the end of the song, Mike "DJ" Valentine rushed back to the microphone and got our attention by clinking a spoon on the side of a champagne glass. "If everyone would grab the beverage of their choice, I would like to toast the newlyweds."

Frank and Dennis scrambled to get all of us a glass of champagne or sparkling cider, and then mission accomplished, Mike continued.

"All of us who know Colleen and Dennis know a little something about how life can throw speed bumps in one's path. Those speed bumps may look different to each of us gathered here today, but we've all managed to either climb over those bumps, or level them in our path."

Dennis tightened his arm around me and kissed my forehead.

Mike started to choke up a bit, but continued. "Sorry, I didn't know I'd get all emotional, but believe me, these are tears of joy. I got to thinking that the start of a life together, such as has occurred today with Dennis and Colleen, is a pure example of hope fulfilled. So with that in mind I'd like to toast the newlyweds with words spoken by writer, Lin Yutang, 'Hope is like a road in the country; there was never a road, but when many people walk on it, the road comes into existence.'

"This room is filled with people who have become close friends, a community of like-minded champions who understand what it means to support others, and to be supported. This toast is for the newlyweds and for all of you in attendance today."

The room was filled with the clinking of glasses as each of us greeted each other in a toast. Dad walked over to Mike and whispered something in his ear, then Mike announced, "And now the father of the bride would like to make a toast."

I sure didn't expect Dad to offer a toast. I hoped for a positive outcome.

Mike held the microphone, and my wonderfully cute father leaned into it and tapped on the mic. "Hello everyone, my name is Patrick Quinn. I'm not a speech maker or anything, but I am the proud father of this young lady, and that's good enough as far as I'm concerned. Being Colleen's father was the crowning glory of my life. I don't know how she's put up with me all these years, but I guess she's just a glutton for punishment."

Oops, there go my tears again; Dennis handed me his handkerchief.

"I don't remember a lot of things, but I do remember a fine Irish toast that seems appropriate for the occasion. Here it goes: 'May the Lord welcome you in Heaven, at least an hour before the Devil knows you're dead.'"

Complete silence permeated the room; a shuffling of feet ensued and nervous coughs emanated from several guests.

Dennis and I both lifted our glasses and added, "Sláinte!" which seemed to give everyone permission to join in the toast with their wishes for our good health.

Mike relieved Dad of the mic and walked him over to Dennis and me. "Sweetie, how'd you like the toast?"

I gave him a hug and a kiss on the cheek, "It was the best toast I've ever received, thank you."

Dennis shook his father-in-law's hand and after Dad whispered something into his ear, my husband ushered him to the men's room for a potty break. I took that opportunity to visit with my family and friends.

. . . . .

Frank felt his phone vibrate in his jacket pocket again and walked away to answer it. "Eddie, are you with Katherine? Is she all right?"

"Yes, she's with me at home now and she's in bed." Eddie walked down the hallway and peaked in on his wife to make sure she was resting. Assured that she couldn't hear him, Eddie returned to the family room and burst into tears.

"Eddie, what else is going on?"

On a sob, Eddie replied, "She doesn't know me at all. It's a miracle I was able to convince her to come home with me. Once we got home she tore off her clothes and went outside to sit on our back patio in her underwear. Nothing I said would convince her to come inside."

"You said she's resting in bed now?"

"Oh yeah, she is, but only after I gave her an anti-anxiety pill with a glass of lemonade. I made an emergency call to Katherine's doctor while she was sitting outside—she wouldn't even let me put a blanket around her—and he suggested I give her one of her anti-anxiety pills."

"I know you've already thought about this, but what about when that pill wears off? What about tomorrow and the next day? You can't just keep sedating her. I mean, what did her doctor suggest you do?"

"Shit, I don't know. Maybe it's time to think about moving her into a facility of some sort . . . I can't believe I just said that."

"Jeez, man, I'm sorry this is happening. What can I do?"

"Can you ask Mike to call me tomorrow? Fill him in on what's happened and tell him I need some direction about next steps for Katherine. This is new territory for me, I could sure use some help."

"I'll do that, but if you think you might start looking at facilities, do you want some company? I can take time off from work to go with you."

"An extra set of eyes would be a real help, yeah. I'll catch up with you once I've talked to Mike and have a clearer idea of where I'm goin' with this entire thing."

Eddie took a seat on his recliner, took a deep breath and felt slightly better than he had at the beginning of the evening. "Hey, how was the wedding?"

"The only way it could have been better is if you and Katherine had been here. The newlyweds should be heading out soon so I guess I'd better go. But Eddie, regardless of the hour, please call if you need to, I'm here for ya'."

"I know that. Thanks."

•   •   •   •   •

Dennis and I went around the room to say our goodbyes. I hugged my dad and told him I'd see him in a few days, then Dennis brought him to The Gazebo where Virgilio would get Dad settled for the night.

Pilar pulled me aside. "Are you sure it's okay that I stay in your condo tonight? What if I get in the way of your sister and brother-in-law?"

"Look, everyone in the family considers you one of us. And besides, you've stayed in my place more often than Patty and Gabe so you can help them get settled on their first night."

I gave Pilar a hug and when I tried to un-hug my best friend, she wouldn't let me go.

"Colleen, I am so happy for you." Then Pilar held me at arm's length. "Looks like you've come full circle now, I mean, gosh, in a few months you'll be moving back into the family home with the absolute perfect guy for you. And oddly enough, I'm still single. What's wrong with this picture?"

"There's nothing wrong with this picture. In all my years of knowing you, you've never implied that without a man your life is a barren wasteland. You've met your fair share of very nice guys. Remember Paul?"

"Boy do I remember Paul. As you would say, yum."

"But time and again you pulled the plug when those nice guys started to make an imprint on your heart and you know Paul imprinted big time. Someone very wise told me about a year ago that it's a good thing to have picky good-guy radar and I think yours is working just fine. What you need, however, is to be ready, willing, and open to being vulnerable."

"I know what you mean, I should have never scared Paul away. My problem is that I'm usually quite ready and willing at the beginning of a relationship . . . if you know what I mean."

"I always know what you mean."

"Right. But then I question whether I might find someone even better." Pilar slapped her own hand in punishment. "Wow, that sounded pretty shallow, didn't it?"

"Not shallow, maybe just overly ambitious. Next time when it's right and you know it, try to imagine how it might feel being with that person the rest of your life. Dennis passed that test with flying colors, some guy will pass your test as well." We said goodbye to each other and Pilar headed to the condo to make sure she hadn't left any of her unmentionables laying around the place.

Sarah came up to say goodbye and knowing how much she'd be interested, I described my honeymoon plans. "Dennis booked a room at the Sorrento Hotel for tonight, and then we're going to Whidbey Island for a couple nights, staying at a place in Greenbank that has rustic, yet romantic, guest cabins. My friend Pilar told me about them."

"I know that place, I read a write-up in The Knot magazine, and the Sorrento Hotel? Sounds like your husband knows how to pick 'em. That hotel happens to be known as one of the most romantic places to stay in downtown Seattle with its city view, massive plush bed, and hot tub."

Sarah is right, I do know how to pick 'em. Dennis returned and we both walked over to my brother and sister. I made sure Patty was clear on the details on where to park at the condo and thanked her and Gabe for taking on doggie sitting duties while Dennis and I were away.

Jonathan updated me on the rental situation with Dad's house. The couple who leased the place last February are aware that Dennis and I will be moving into the house at the end of their lease period and they agreed to vacate the house by the middle of January. That gives me time to put my place on the market in the hopes that my Queen Anne condo sells right away so Dennis and I can buy and move into the family home in Wallingford. Truth be told, the family is relieved that the house didn't sell to a new buyer. Keeping the home in the family feels right, and Dennis and I will take real good care of it for Mom and Dad.

THIRTY-SIX

Dennis and I already celebrated Thanksgiving with Dad at The Gazebo's pre-holiday meal four days earlier, but we both felt the on-the-day celebration wouldn't be the same without him so we picked Dad up at three o'clock on Thursday and headed to Jonathan and Melanie's house. Dad had a vague recollection of having already celebrated some sort of winter holiday and wondered if today was Christmas. I explained that the holiday he remembered was Thanksgiving but we all liked turkey and fixings so much, we decided to eat it again.

My nephew Kirby was home on break from Washington State University. As if I needed proof of how unpredictable Alzheimer's is, Dad still had no inkling of Jonathan and Melanie's identities but he warmed up to his grandson, even greeting him as such when we first arrived at their house. And even though the hosts for this evening may as well be strangers in his eyes, he approved of the people I chose to call my friends and was happy to be a dinner guest at their home.

Jonathan came up with a pretty keen idea: he and Melanie would address Dad as Patrick, rather than Dad, to avoid any unnecessary confusion on his part. Strangely, Dad mentioned that Jonathan looked familiar to him, but he didn't know from where. I knew Jonathan visited him at least once—at least that time last June was the only incident of which I was aware.

Dennis and Jonathan have become pretty tight in the last few months. I didn't know the source of that connection but I was glad for it. Of course Melanie and I remained very close, and although our get-togethers happened less frequently, we still managed to keep up-to-date on what's what and who's who.

She and I went into the kitchen to put the finishing touches on the

Thanksgiving meal.

"Thanks for hosting this dinner. Dad was glad to have another holiday meal even though in his mind it's not Thanksgiving Day since he already celebrated that with Dennis and me at The Gazebo a few days ago."

"Oh, that's right, Jonathan told me about that. He said he saw posters about the dinner at the front desk of the facility's lobby the beginning of November."

Huh? How would my brother know anything about that? "You say he was at the facility the beginning of this month?"

"Right, why?"

"I guess I'm just surprised to hear that he was there more than once." I saw the look of confusion on Melanie's face and I tried to clear it up.

"Okay, I'll let you in on a secret. I saw him sitting down and talking with Dad back in June but I didn't tell Jonathan that I had seen him. I figured if he wanted to keep the visit a secret, I sure wasn't gonna ruin it for him."

"Colleen, Jonathan has visited Patrick almost every week starting this past summer. I thought you knew that. Dennis knows, he's talked to Jonathan several times when he was there to visit your dad." Melanie threw her hand over her mouth. "Crap. You didn't know. That means Dennis didn't tell you."

"No, he didn't." I peeked into the living room and saw Kirby sitting with his grandpa, and Jonathan and Dennis laughing it up across the room. I turned back to Melanie who had a frantic look on her face.

"I think I blew it. I assumed since Dennis knew, you did too. Are you mad?"

"I have a feeling my husband and your husband struck a gentleman's agreement regarding this matter. I'm disappointed my brother didn't feel comfortable telling me about it—not that we talk with each other all that much—but that's my fault as much as his. I'm glad Jonathan has started to include Dad in his life."

I hugged Melanie. "It's all good. No harm, no foul, but why don't we keep their gentleman's agreement a secret for a while longer."

As a result of this revelation, the evening took on even greater significance for me. I had much for which to be thankful—my *Things I'm Grateful for List* having grown to epic proportions even with Dad's disease downturn—but this Thanksgiving I had a new item to add to the list: Jonathan was coming around and both he and Dad would benefit as a result.

· · · · ·

On the way back to the condo, Dennis and I were content to ride in silence. I thought back to our wedding dance and about something my new husband had said in response to my confession that I needed to be more patient with Jonathan. He said that baby steps were better than none, that maybe it wouldn't take as long as I thought it would. Of course now all of that made perfect sense.

I looked over at Dennis who must have felt my eyes on him because he briefly turned his head towards me, smiled, and turned his attention back to the road. I looked through my side window so he wouldn't see the tears that pooled in my eyes—happy tears to be sure, but tears nonetheless.

THIRTY-SEVEN

Four score and seven years ago, Patrick Craig Quinn was born to Irish immigrant parents. My grandfather's family name, Quinn, means intelligent; Dad's first name, nobly born; his middle name means rock. If ever a combination of names fit the description of a person to a T, Patrick Craig Quinn was that combination. At eighty-seven, Dad still had his wits about him; able to think quickly—albeit not as quick as a few years ago—and he was somewhat capable of reacting to things he didn't expect. I didn't anticipate, however, that he wouldn't remember my name when I picked him up for his birthday dinner. He easily rolled with the punches when his caregiver, Virgilio, told him his daughter was there to pick him up for dinner, by greeting my friendly face with a resounding, "Happy Birthday to me, my daughter."

At first, I didn't think anything of it; he'd certainly talked to and about me without using my name before, but part way through dinner—which we hosted at our Wallingford house where we grew up and where he and Mom resided for forty years—Dad leaned into me and said, "It's been nice meeting you today and having this birthday celebration at your lovely home. Have you and your husband lived here long?"

I had reviewed the GDS brochure so many times in the past two years, I knew the seven stages of his disease by heart. This was the one aspect of the sixth stage that was lacking: Dad forgetting who I was. Everyone at the table heard Dad's comment. Silence prevailed until my nephew started to correct my dad. "Grandpa, that's your—"

Melanie jumped up from the table. "Kirby, could you help me with the dishes? I need you in the kitchen. Now." My poor nephew hadn't a clue as to what the big deal was. Grandpa forgot his aunt's name, Kirby simply wanted to remind him of it. Jonathan caught his son's attention and gave a quick head shake and gestured for him to join his mom in the kitchen.

Dennis rubbed my leg under the table which broke me out of my numbed-state. "I'm glad you like the house, Patrick. My husband and I moved in here not too long ago. We purchased it from a family who lived here almost their entire lives."

Dad looked around at what he could see of the house from his viewpoint. "I bet a lot of memories were created here. Ya' don't live in a place for a long time without doing that."

Dennis squeezed my thigh. "That's true. I heard that an extraordinary family lived here before us, and that many wonderful years were spent within these walls. Colleen and I feel privileged being able to take over the house for the family."

"Colleen did you say? That's a fine Irish girl's name. You know, don't you, that your name means 'girl' so I guess no one was confused at your birth whether you were a lass or a lad."

Suddenly this evening became very surreal and uncomfortable for me but I had to say something. I glanced at Jonathan and managed to say, "That's very true, and my father told me that when he and my mother chose my middle name, they both secretly wrote their choice of name on a slip of paper. When they turned over their individual choices, they had written the same name."

"Now what name was that?"

"Fiona. My mother and father chose the name Fiona for my middle name."

Dad looked up at the ceiling, then down at the table, then back at me. "Colleen Fiona. That has a nice ring to it, I like it very much. Can I call you Colleen Fiona?"

"I'd be honored, and so would my parents."

"Then Colleen Fiona it is. And what's your husband's name again?"

Dennis reached across the table to shake Dad's hand. "My name is Dennis Stewart McGee, it's a pleasure to meet you."

"So that would make you Colleen Fiona McGee . . . there's nothing wrong with combining the Irish with the Scottish, nothing wrong at all."

Dennis and I offered to take Dad back to The Gazebo and we asked Dad if it would be okay to visit him from time to time and invite him back to our home for a meal or two in the future. He thought that was a grand idea, which was good, because there's no way Colleen Fiona would ever stay away.

. . . . .

While we were gone, Jonathan and Melanie finalized the post-dinner cleanup and locked up the house for us, securing Ramona in the laundry room because she needed a bit more time to get accustomed to her new home before being given free rein of the place. My nephew Kirby left to stay at a friend's house before his return to Washington State University the following morning. I was so impressed that he made the five hour drive from Eastern Washington just to be in Seattle for his grandpa's birthday. If Melanie or Jonathan didn't explain why his grandpa forgot my name, I would make a point of doing so the next time I talked to him.

When we got back to our newly acquired family home in Wallingford, Dennis and I took Ramona for a walk and then over a mug of green tea, we downloaded the happenings of the evening.

"Do you think I'm gone forever in Dad's eyes? I mean, is it possible this was just a fluke and the next time he'll remember me?"

Dennis sat on the couch behind me while I sat on the floor in front of him—he knew I carried tension in my shoulders and neck so he made every effort to massage it away. "Knowing how unpredictable things are, I'm not certain how to answer that. I guess emotionally, you should prepare for the worst."

There was Patty's philosophy rearing its ugly head again. "So I guess I need to stay armed for bear from now on." I turned around towards Dennis and laid my head on his knee. "I don't want to, I don't wanna be armed at all where Dad is concerned." Then I let it all out.

Dennis lifted me up onto the couch, put his arms around me, and leaned me into his chest. Ramona took up the position I just vacated and placed her head on Dennis's knee while I had a quintessential Colleen crying jag.

Dennis let me cry, choosing to just be present while I mourned the loss of an identity connection with my dad. When my crying slowed to a whimper, he reminded me of Victoria's situation when her husband forgot who she was and how everyone agreed that not knowing the connection didn't make the relationship any less vital.

Intellectually, I knew I was still Patrick Quinn's daughter, but my heart had quite a bit of catching-up to do. Now I knew how it must have felt when both my brother and sister became just another friendly face as far as our dad was concerned. I owed them a huge apology for not being more sympathetic at the time.

I continued to consider this disease a moving target. One day the target stayed still and a status quo seemed likely; the next day—or even the next hour—the target resumed its uncatchable and erratic path. All I needed to do was go with the flow, regardless of how strong the current.

Seems doable, I guess, unless I get swept downstream and over the falls.

THIRTY-EIGHT

Dennis left the house for a volunteer dinner sponsored by the VA so I settled onto my loveseat with Ramona and a glass of merlot and gave my Whidbey friend a call. The first words out of her mouth shocked me. I couldn't help my response. "Don't give me that, you met someone?"

"You shouldn't act so surprised, I've still got game."

"I'm not sure what that means in relation to someone our age but if it means you still have the ability to attract a man, I agree with you. Give me all the deets and don't leave anything out."

So this is how the meet-and-greet took place. Pilar had just finished teaching a knitting class at her store when an older lady entered accompanied by a tall, salt and pepper-haired man. As Pilar described it, their eyes met and it was Kismet. I knew a little something about instant connections with the opposite sex—thank you Dennis—but I was interested in how my friend fared during her exchange.

"I couldn't help myself, Colleen. I walked right up to the woman and the Adonis, looked right over the head of the old gal and extended my hand in greeting. Good god, I almost knocked the hat right off the lady's head."

"You didn't."

"I'm afraid so, but once the Adonis straightened the woman's hat, he greeted me and said his mother was looking for a very special type of yarn and was certain a fine store like mine had it in stock. He actually said, 'a fine store like mine.'"

"Well, you do sell yarn, it's not a stretch to assume you had a wide variety of the stuff."

"Stop that! Don't you go and change my interpretation of what happened."

I apologized and told her to continue.

"Turns out I had the yarn she was looking for and I carried it in six different color combinations. His momma told me it would take some time for her to decide on which color to buy so she sat down on one of the comfy chairs in the nook section of the store—you know, the corner seating area where—"

"Pilar, I've been to your store numerous times, I know what it looks like."

"Sorry, so anyway, while she examined the skeins of yarn, Adonis and I got to talking. Oh, his name is Jack, Jack Pritchard."

"So does Jack-Jack Pritchard's mother have a name?"

"I'm sure she does but I don't remember it. Any who, then his mom wanted to look at some of the patterns I sell—you know, the ones on the racks near the classroom area?"

"Pilar . . ."

"Oh, right, you've seen 'em. Okay, so now we're talking real friendly-like and fortunately the part-time gal I hired was on duty that day so she handled the customers, and before I knew it, I had a dinner date."

"And how did that go?"

"That dinner went well, and so did dinner a couple days later at his place, and so did drinks and dinner at my place last night."

"Wait a minute. You've known this guy for several days now and you didn't call to tell me? If I hadn't called you tonight, how long would it have taken for you to give me a holler?"

"You're right, I'm a terrible best friend, but when I met him I had just come off a visit from my sister—you know, the one who lives in Portland? That really steered me way off track—"

"I can well imagine."

"So you understand why I've been out-of-touch. Forgive me?"

"Of course I do, but tell me more about the guy other than the fact that he looks like the god of beauty and desire."

"He gets me, Colleen. We laugh at the same things, he thinks it's great that I have my own business and I'm doing what I love to do, and he likes to cook and tries out new recipes from cooking shows, just like you do."

"Congratulations, you've met the male version of me!"

Silence from Pilar, then more silence. "I think you have a point there, but you could never turn me on like this guy does. Have mercy, you could never pull that off."

"Point taken, but how come you haven't seen this guy before? I would have thought your guy radar would have found him long before now."

"You know that's true. You see, he moved on-island last month with his mother. Well, she moved into a senior apartment community and he moved into a home of his own—thank the Universe—so with him getting his mama settled in, there was no chance of our paths crossing. Oh, and he's a journalist and looking to start a book club at Whidbey Island Books. He reads!"

I couldn't contain myself and burst out laughing, startling Ramona which caused her to jump off the loveseat and look at me with concerned eyes. I assured her with a rub between her ears. "Pilar, it sure sounds like you've found a winner. He helps his momma, he's a writer, he cooks, and he can read. Say no more, I'm sold."

And I definitely was. I knew she'd find the right guy when the time was right and it sure looked like she had. I hope this guy is Mr. Right; that type of wonderfulness happening to my best friend would be the crowning achievement in my hoping and praying that a guy would fall into her very worthy net.

THIRTY-NINE

Dennis and I rode to the caregiver support meeting together because we were going from there to The Gazebo to visit Dad. Just as Mike started the meeting, that young girl, Grace, walked into the room, stood just inside the door and said, "My dad died. He's gone from this earth and I don't care."

I turned to Dennis and raised my eyebrows and thought, *now there's an opener.* Mike stood and walked over to the thirty-something-year-old member of our meeting and extended a hug to her. She didn't hug back; she stood there with her arms dangling from her sides and then abruptly stepped away from the facilitator.

"I don't need, or want, any sympathy, I just thought the group should know this will be my last meeting."

Grace sat in the empty seat next to Victoria whose hug for Grace seemed to be scrambling to get out. "Grace, dear, I don't know quite how to say it, but was this . . . outcome . . . somewhat sudden?"

"Yep, it was. I already told everyone that he had diabetes, was an alcoholic most of his adult life, and had a heart condition. Well, it's the heart that did him in. Massive heart attack yesterday. I called my sister Cynthia to tell her, and she greeted the news with, 'Ding dong the bastard is dead. Praise the Lord, the bastard is dead.' I guess that pretty much sums it all up."

If everyone was thinking the way I was, we weren't certain how to respond to this news about the death of a man who sexually abused his two daughters. I put in my two cents worth. "I'm sure you're still digesting all that's happened." I gestured to the group around the table. "Is there anything we can do for you? Do you need help with his funeral arrangements?"

"Hah! Don't get me wrong, that's real nice of you to offer, but there won't be any service. He'll be cremated—Cynthia said she'll go halfsies on the cost of it—and that's all there is to it. Case closed."

Grace crossed her arms in front of her. "Next!"

Whoa, how do you follow that bit of news? Rose did the honors. "I have something good to report, if that's okay."

"Yes, please," a simultaneous utterance from several of us around the table.

"As you know, Sophia has been pretty much uncommunicative since she had her stroke. The nursing home where she lives tried everything to get some sort of reaction or response to her surroundings—and God knows Gabe and I tried. Turns out, the administration of the building took on the *Alive Inside* program to help its residents. Do you know the program I'm talking about?"

Dennis and I had but we weren't all that familiar with it. "When the *Alive Inside* movie was in Seattle, Colleen and I considered seeing it but during the few days it was here, we just couldn't fit it into our schedule."

Rose continued. "I *did* see the movie but didn't know if that type of therapy—they call it *Music and Memory*—would help my sister. I mean she's been totally removed from life as we know it since her stroke. So anyway, what they do is ask the family member to create a personalized music list, for example, music that Sophia would have listened to prior to her stroke. That song list is put into a computer database and transferred into an iPod which the patient listens to with a set of headphones. The hope is that the personalized music—something that most people can no doubt tie memories to—will awaken something within the patient as well."

Mike commented that he had heard it was a very worthwhile program that was well-documented to be very beneficial to those with cognitive impairment.

"I can tell you, it worked for Sophia. I was there when they first put the headphones on her head. She was just sitting in a recliner next to her bed, not moving at all, not engaging with me or anyone else for that matter. I chose the first song for her to listen to and about a minute into it her right foot started to move from side to side and then she started to kind-of, sort-of sing: 'Next phase, new wave, dance craze, anyways, it's still rock and roll to me.' It was pretty hard to understand what she was singing but in my mind it was the real deal.

Can you believe it?"

Victoria thought it was grand. "Do you think it would work with Frank Sinatra or Cab Calloway songs? Maybe my George would enjoy that too."

"I'm sure it would work for him. Billy Joel was one of Sophia's favorite singers so that's the music that did it for her. The same thing should work for George, Katherine, Patrick, and anyone else, right Mike?"

"It's worth a try. If the facility where your loved one lives hasn't officially signed up with the program, you can fill an iPod with music that meets the tastes of your loved one and implement the therapy yourself. And of course, those of you with family members still at home can do the same on your own. I feel remiss in not telling you about it but I'm glad Rose witnessed the transformation first-hand and could describe it to us."

Rose nodded. "I'm not naïve, my sister is still a victim of a stroke, but listening to familiar music gives her a chance to be reactive and to come out of the shell the stroke put her in more than a year ago. I'm thrilled with the transformation, but what's more important is that she's personally benefitting from the program. Imagine, something as simple as music improving her quality of life."

Dennis had a brainstorm. "Victoria, months ago at the senior center dance, your husband knew dance steps to a Cab Calloway song that he must have learned years and years ago, yet he seemed to know what he was doing. Did he?"

"Oh yes he did. I hadn't thought about it, but you're right. His recollection of those dance steps far surpassed his memory of anything else going on at the time. It must have been the music. What a nice memory, thank you for reminding me of it."

Dennis nodded his head and took my hand.

I said, "I have to tell you, this story made my day. I needed to hear some positive news today . . . I know Grace that your news wasn't positive at all, I didn't mean your news was positive, but Rose's music story kind of balances out some of the not-so-great stuff going on with the group. Thank you Rose."

Dennis turned to Frank. "How's my buddy, Sean, doing?"

Frank took off his Sounders soccer cap and placed it gently on the table. "Thanks for asking, he's doing okay. You remember how depressed he was when you first started working with him?"

"I do, he was not a happy camper."

"To say the least, but at the Veterans group that he attends, he's kind of taken on a leadership role. Not an official title mind you, but the head of the group told me that Sean watches out for the other guys. I guess you could say he's a mentor of sorts."

"I'm very happy to hear that. I knew all along that in time he'd turn the corner and be able to give as much as he receives. He's a good soldier, and a good man."

"Thanks, Dennis."

When Dennis and I left the meeting, I realized I hadn't participated as much as I had in the past. I hadn't run out of stories to tell, and probably never would, but my need for this meeting wasn't as great as it had been before. I was content just to be present and listen to everyone else. I guess that's a step in the right direction—at least I hoped it was.

FORTY

When it came to doing activities in downtown Seattle, I missed living on Queen Anne hill. Tonight, Dennis and I are meeting Jonathan and Melanie at Purple Café and Wine Bar. If we were still living at the condo we would have walked or taken a quick bus ride to the restaurant instead of driving in from Wallingford. We lucked out, however, and found an inexpensive parking spot four blocks from the restaurant. My brother was the host for the dinner and told me that he reserved a table in a semi-private area of the restaurant.

Dennis hadn't eaten at the Café yet and was looking forward to doing so. I was glad to participate in this novel dining experience with him. Hugs were exchanged and then we got down to business, ordering wine. Purple Café stocks some of the finest local and global wines; I've never tasted a Purple wine with which I didn't instantly fall in love. Jonathan chose an Andrew Januik Stone Cairn cabernet sauvignon that left a fine impression on me. My first impression, yum! My second impression, smooth and absolutely memorable.

After we placed our dinner orders Jonathan spoke an over-used but applicable line for the evening. "I guess you're wondering why I called you here today."

I did kind of wonder, I couldn't recall the last time I dined with my brother outside of one of our homes. "Is it because you and Melanie were afraid the two of you wouldn't be able to finish a bottle of wine by yourselves and needed our help?"

"Not at all."

Jonathan glanced at Melanie who nodded in encouragement, then he looked directly at me. "A little bird told me that you're aware that I've been visiting Dad every week for almost a year now."

Dennis held up his hands in surrender. "Dude, I promise, I didn't say a word."

"I know you didn't. When you saw me at The Gazebo the first time, I was pretty embarrassed because I hadn't exactly been a very warm and supportive family member towards Dad."

Too bad I was sipping my wine during that admission, I choked on that unfortunate sip. I guzzled down half a glass of water and said, "Sorry, must have sipped too fast, go on."

Jonathan knew better. "Truthfully? I was a total prick. When Dad was first diagnosed with Alzheimer's, if I could have hidden from the entire family I would have."

He took Melanie's hand in his. "This tenacious wife of mine wouldn't let me. Trust me, it's not like I didn't realize that my actions were callous and shallow. I did, but I had no interest in changing because I didn't want to accept the whole damn crap-fest. If I didn't accept it, it wouldn't be real."

I started to say something but Jonathan didn't let me. "I know. Denial. I get it. That was my escape route and it's a route on which Melanie never let me get comfortable. If you think it was easy coexisting with this woman during that time, you're sorely mistaken."

I lifted my wine glass toward Melanie and she lifted hers. "Way to go, Melanie!"

That broke the tension and gave all of us an excuse to relax and sit back in our chairs. "Can I say something now?"

Jonathan put down his wine glass and said, "Sure."

"Several months after Dad moved in, I saw you at The Gazebo visiting with him. I'm ashamed to say I also eavesdropped on your conversation. I shouldn't have, but darn it, I was witness to an unexpected event in your relationship with him and I wasn't about to bail. I didn't let on that I saw you because I wanted you to continue your visits with Dad and was afraid to get in the way of that."

This time I took a slow sip of my wine. "What hurt, however, was that you felt it necessary to keep it a secret, that you didn't feel comfortable telling me about it. I have a part in that, and—"

"And so do I. Once a prick, always a prick."

"Oh shut up. Once a prick doesn't mean you can't change, you've already proved that."

"Thanks, and thank you for everything you've done for Dad, and everything you're still doing."

Wow, this was a two-for-one night: Dennis tried a new restaurant and my brother and I were being accommodating to each other. With perfect timing, the waitress delivered our entrees as follows: Maine Lobster Mac and Cheese for me, Filet Mignon for Dennis, Grilled Wild King Salmon for Melanie, and Braised Lamb Tagine for Jonathan. My hubby and I were happy with each other's choices—after all, we'd be switching plates half way through. Melanie liked my way of dining and managed to convince my brother to do the same. He conceded that it was a great idea because he'd get to enjoy two different meals in one sitting.

I'm always willing to take credit for great ideas, and this one was one of my tastiest.

FORTY-ONE

With Dad being so well cared for by The Gazebo staff, I rarely check my cell phone while at work. The relief of turning my overwrought and concern-filled brain over to people who can address those concerns is a luxury I've enjoyed for close to two years now. I can't say enough about how wonderful it has been to be a daughter instead of an active caregiver. I know Dad's financial situation affords me that privilege, and I also know there are untold numbers of unpaid caregivers without similar financial means who are still on 24/7 duty where their loved ones are concerned. Up until this point my family has encountered speed bumps, but nothing like what other caregivers face on an ongoing basis.

Then a huge bump in the road appeared that threatened to crumple the status quo in which I had mistakenly taken comfort. It came in the guise of my sister-in-law unexpectedly showing up at the bridal salon. Evidently the Health & Wellness Director at The Gazebo tried to reach me on my cell and on our store's phone line, but both options went to voicemail. Melanie walked through the door of the salon just as I was finalizing a sale with a customer.

I smiled warmly at my brother's wife. "Oops, did I forget a lunch date or something? What day is it?"

"No lunch date, I'm here because The Gazebo tried to reach you and failing that, called Jonathan. Your dad is in the hospital."

"Whoa, what are you talking about? Did he fall or something?"

Melanie told the entire dreary story. Shortly after my dad woke up, he complained of a sharp pain in his groin area. The caregiver helped him to the toilet and got him dressed for breakfast, hoping that relieving his bladder, and moving about the unit, might lessen the level of pain; it only worsened. Jonathan was able to take Dad to the Emergency Room so our dad didn't have to go through the stress of being transported by a medical vehicle. He didn't recognize Jonathan, but at least my brother was a friendly face and the staff assured Dad he was in good hands.

• • • • •

When I arrived at his bedside in the ER, Dad looked utterly confused. "I don't know why I'm here. Have you come to take me home?"

Jonathan left me alone with Dad and joined Melanie in the waiting area. "Patrick, I'm happy to see you again, but this isn't what I had in mind. I hear you're having some pain down below, is it real bad?"

Dad looked at me and squinted. "You're that nice person who visits me."

"Yes, that's me, Colleen Fiona."

"What a lovely Irish name—" He didn't finish his statement, instead he let out a scream that got immediate attention by the staff.

"Mr. Quinn, are you okay?"

"Jesus, Mary and Joseph I hurt like the dickens. Why do I hurt?"

"That's what we're trying to find out. Would you like something for the pain?"

I threw my hands in the air. "Of course he wants something for the pain, he didn't scream for the hell of it!"

"And you are?"

I pulled the doctor outside the cubicle while a nurse remained with my dad. "I'm his daughter, Colleen McGee, the sister of the man who brought my dad here from the facility. My father has Alzheimer's—"

"Yes, we have his medical paperwork that traveled with him. Your father is very agitated, I'd like to give him a sedative."

I read the doctor's name tag. "Dr. . . . Becker, he's agitated because he's in a lot of pain. I'm sure once his pain is relieved he'll calm down considerably."

"I've ordered a low-dose narcotic pain reliever for him, he'll be getting that soon."

"Will that be enough?"

"I understand that you want your father to be comfortable but we have to guard against his cognition level becoming even more compromised than it already is. We need him to be able to communicate what he's feeling. Additionally, a lower dose lessens the risk of respiratory depression in patients of your father's age."

I must not have looked appeased because the doctor continued. "We're going to catheterize your father to reduce the pressure in the bladder area which should bring him considerable relief. We're also going to test his urine to see if the antibiotics he's been on for the past week have done anything towards getting rid of his urinary tract infection. Your father will also have a prostate exam and an ultrasound to determine if there are other complications."

"Other complications? He's been on a prostate medication for some time now and he hasn't had any reoccurrence of prostate issues . . . except perhaps, right now?"

"We'll let the pain medication take effect before we do those two tests. If those tests are inconclusive, he'll need a CAT scan."

"Do what you need to do as long as you make him more comfortable. I want him to get home—back to The Gazebo—as soon as possible. He'll be happier there."

"We'll see what we can do."

• • • • •

The staff did what they could to make Dad comfortable, and to make him better, with little effect. Nothing I said or did made a difference either. Four hours after he arrived at the hospital Dad was taken to a patient room while Jonathan, Dennis, and I sat with the ER doctor to discuss his case. Dad's urinary tract infection was clearing up but his prostate was enlarged so that it extended into the bladder. There was gross blood in his urine and inflammatory changes in the bladder wall as a result of the infection. The doctor saved the worst for last: Dad had a pretty nasty-looking tumor in the prostate, a significant reason why it was so enlarged.

Dr. Becker showed us the CAT Scan which revealed a walnut-sized tumor. Now all his complaints about discomfort "down there" made sense. The next day, an oncologist met with us, Dad was also present, and the doctor advised that any treatments, most notably surgery, were not an option because Dad's body was too frail to undergo an onslaught of any kind. We understood the logic in the doctor's counsel but it was extremely difficult not doing anything substantive to treat his prostate cancer. Dad's health care directive made that decision a bit easier.

Several years ago—prior to having compromised cognition—Dad specifically stated in the directive that if he was diagnosed with a terminal condition and no curative treatments were appropriate, he wanted palliative measures put in place, nothing more. The family and I had only one option available to us: do whatever we could to help Dad make it through the remaining days of his life.

Two days later, Dad left the hospital with a prescription for a low dose narcotic. The narcotic caused constipation that was somewhat relieved by a laxative cocktail a couple times a day. Over the next two weeks, his cognition level definitely declined, but even after all the trauma he'd been through, he still maintained his sense of humor and his gentlemanly demeanor. I hoped that type of calm was carried in the genes because there was no way I would be able to pull it off should I find myself in a similar situation somewhere down the road.

• • • • •

I kept in touch with my sister by phone to keep her current on Dad's health status. Patty wanted to know if she should make a trip to Seattle, the unspoken question being whether this development was going to be the catalyst for Dad's demise. No one knew the answer to that, although we all suspected he was approaching the end of his journey.

Of one thing all of us were certain: Alzheimer's disease, and Dad's age, made getting well an impossibility. Being eighty-seven years of age can be a deterrent to receiving cancer treatments, but it doesn't have to be. We were convinced Alzheimer's disease would be the true cause of death where our father was concerned.

Knowing that Dad's life was balanced precariously over the edge, I again reduced my work hours so I could spend more time with him. Sarah assured me the salon should be the least of my concerns; if I wanted to show up for work, that would be fine, but if I didn't or couldn't, that was okay too.

FORTY-TWO

Dad's health took a drastic turn after his stay in the hospital the previous month. He was weak due to both the urinary tract infection and the prostate tumor, but for all intents and purposes, initially he seemed alert, albeit in considerable pain. He didn't understand all that was going on while he was in the hospital, but he understood enough of what the hospital oncologist had explained about treatment options, that he stated very clearly that he wanted nothing more than to be home in his own bed.

Three weeks after leaving the hospital his pain became so severe he was prescribed a stronger narcotic—morphine placed in his mouth with a dropper—that eventually rendered him unconscious most of the time. In addition to not wanting any aggressive or extraordinary measures to extend his life, he opted out of invasive methods of hydration and nutrition as well. Knowing that his pain medication was going to be increased, Dad requested that that element of his directive be put into place. The family's top priority was to keep Dad comfortable even though the increased morphine could hasten his death. There was no way we would allow him to suffer during whatever time he had left.

Once Dad returned to The Gazebo, his primary caregiver, Virgilio, removed the dresser from Dad's room and added a cot and two additional chairs for visitors. I had virtually camped out at Dad's bedside, catching a few winks here and there, but for the most part I just sat and talked to him, believing he'd hear whatever I had to say.

Dennis spent part of each day with me and encouraged—and only partially succeeded—in getting me out of the building as much as possible while he stayed with Dad. He also brought a few changes of clothes for me and forced me into Dad's shower to freshen up so I could feel slightly human again. The Sergeant ministered to me, while

I ministered to my dad; it was a system that ushered me through some very difficult days.

A few days ago, I made an emergency call to St. Benedicts Catholic Church to ask a priest to give Dad last rights, I guess they call it Anointing of the Sick now. Dad's long-standing attendance at St. Benedicts gave him priority status—a priest showed up that same day. Jonathan wasn't able to be at Dad's bedside for that anointing—he and Melanie were in Los Angeles at a conference—but they left LA later that day, knowing Dad didn't have too many days remaining. I wonder if Mom observed that anointing from her vantage point—it was so precious.

. . . . .

Father Joseph Morrison, a retired priest who appeared to be in his late 70's, explained the Anointing of the Sick before he carried out the solemn ritual given to my dad, a life-long Catholic who would soon depart this life. I took great comfort in the ritual, and never took my eyes off Dad. He had made it very clear in his end-of-life requests that he wanted a priest to do the deed when it appeared he didn't have much longer to live. It was an honor to fulfill that wish.

I hadn't gone to Mass since Dad and I stopped visiting Mom, but hearing Father Morrison recite the Latin prayers took me back to all those Sundays when Mom and Dad required attendance at Mass unless us kids were sick with fever. We came up with so many excuses not to go—ingrown toenails, a splinter in a finger, a tip-of-the-nose pimple—but nothing worked. I smiled at the memory, a smile that turned into a sob when I focused back on Father Morrison who led me in the Lord's Prayer at the conclusion of the ritual. Once completed I asked the kind priest if he had done everything my father would have wanted. He assured me that all was well and told me that during his vespers that evening, he would pray for me, my father, and the remainder of the family.

. . . . .

Now two days later, Patty is arriving from California and Jonathan will pick her up at the airport and bring her to The Gazebo. I continued to remain at Dad's beside where he had been a captive audience to my never-ending chatter. I insisted Dennis keep to his schedule at the Veterans Hospital because right at that moment, there was nothing he could do for Dad and I needed some alone time with him anyway. Until Jonathan and Patty arrived, I was happy it was just Dad and me.

I sat as close as possible to him and in my best imitation of singing on key, I sang him an Irish tune that he loved, a song he used to sing to Mom when he had to leave Seattle to go on a business trip.

Red is the rose that in yonder garden grows
Fair is the lily of the valley
Clear is the water that flows from the Boyne
But my love is fairer than any.

Come over the hills, my bonnie Irish lass
Come over the hills to your darling
You choose the rose, love, and I'll make the vow
And I'll be your true love forever.

Virgilio Sandoval, caregiver extraordinaire, entered the room just as I finished. "That's a beautiful song, I'm certain your father heard you loud and clear. Although Patrick is unconscious, he's comfortable."

"He does look at peace, doesn't he?"

"Most definitely, and we're doing all we can to keep him that way. While you're visiting with him, if you see him grimace, or his forehead crease, let me know and we'll give him some additional morphine."

I patted Dad's forehead, smoothed down his hair, and responded, "You've been so kind to me and my father. When he was still able, my dad told me how much he liked and respected you. We really lucked out when you were assigned to his care."

"He's a fine man that father of yours, it truly has been my pleasure." Virgilio grabbed a tissue from the nightstand and wiped his eyes. "Will other family members be visiting as well?"

"Yes, I expect they'll arrive soon. Could you bring my brother and sister into Dad's room when they arrive? In the interim, is there anything else I can do to make him more comfortable?"

"One thing you can do is put a cold, wet washcloth on his forehead and another one over his feet. Keep refreshing the washcloths as they get room temperature. He has a fever because his body is gradually shutting down and it's been awhile since he's had any liquids. I have to ask this, so forgive me. You're aware that his Advanced Health Care Directive specifically states no nutrition and no hydration, correct?"

"I know that document forwards and backwards and I'm thrilled Dad had the foresight years ago to put one in place. I'm sure you're aware, that's one of the reasons why cancer treatment isn't an option for him. He was very specific in his documented wishes about what he wanted and didn't want if he was diagnosed with a terminal illness."

I paused to collect myself. "Well, I guess Alzheimer's qualifies as a terminal illness on its own."

I held Dad's hand and gazed into his face. "I'm sure you're very busy Virgilio. Thank you for the cooling down suggestion relating to his fever, I'll pamper him like he deserves."

Ministering to Dad was a blessing, I was glad to have an opportunity to do something extra for him. I enjoyed talking to him, and I continued to hope he was taking it all in. "You were the best father a daughter could have. You were so good to Mom, and so supportive of each of us kids. We had a great family experience and we're so lucky to have had Mom for as long as we did and to have enjoyed you for an additional seven years. I wish you could be around longer, but I want you to know, it's okay to go. I bet Mom's already beckoning you to join her. No doubt she has some heaven improvement projects for you to complete."

I chuckled at a memory. "Remember when you were in the hospital a month ago? You were sick, but you were still with it. I read somewhere that it's important to let a dying person know that they can leave—that they have permission to go. So when I said that you didn't have to stay—that you should feel free to go—you responded, 'Where are we going? Is it time to go home?' I thought that was so cute, and I kind of felt embarrassed for jumping the gun by prematurely giving you the end-of-life-permission-to-leave statement. But I'm quite certain that now is the correct time for me to tell you that it's okay for you to go. I know Jonathan and Patty would say the same thing."

I wiped the tears from my face, looked at my watch, and said, "By the way, they should be here real soon. I'll go out in the hallway and call them to see how far away they are."

No sooner had I entered the hallway than I saw Virgilio escorting my brother and sister down the hall. After tight hugs, I filled them in. "Don't be shocked when you see Dad. His breathing is very ragged now. You'll hear him take a gravelly breath, and then nothing, and then another desperate sounding breath. Virgilio said that's normal because the time between breaths is getting longer, and the breaths are getting shallower. This type of breathing started last night, that's why Paula, the Health & Wellness Director, suggested the family be nearby as soon as possible."

I slapped myself on the side of my head. "What am I saying, you already know all that, that's why you're here. Anyway, I told Dad you were both on the way, so let's go in and see him."

We surrounded the bed. "Hey Dad, look what the cat dragged in, Jonathan and Patty are here." I advised my siblings to speak loudly and lean in close so Dad could hear them.

"Hi Dad, it's Patty. I'm so glad I'm here."

"Dad? Jonathan. I love you so much."

I noticed that I hadn't heard any ragged breathing sounds since we entered the room so I placed my hands lightly on Dad's chest. A minute later I tried to hold it together when I told my siblings that our dad was no longer breathing.

"No! Dad, it's Patty! I'm here . . . so is Jonathan!" I hugged my sister and told her I was sorry. With that she ran out of the room.

Jonathan dropped to his knees and put his head on the bed. "I should've gotten here sooner. I didn't say goodbye."

I joined Jonathan on the floor and placed an arm around his shoulders. "I'm sorry for that, I truly am, but you said your visit the other day was a good one, that Dad was even awake for part of it."

I pulled Jonathan's face toward mine and said, "Look at me . . .

didn't you say Dad's old sense of humor was alive and kicking, and that you were able to share some laughs? I think that particular goodbye counted more than one you could have said today."

"Yeah, but it wasn't enough, it was never enough."

I excused myself and walked out to the hallway and asked Virgilio to confirm Dad's passing. He placed the stethoscope on Dad's heart and listened for a few seconds; he then moved the stethoscope around the chest cavity. He draped the stethoscope over the back of his neck and said, "Your wonderful father has passed. He's resting peacefully now."

I asked Virgilio to call the funeral home to make arrangements to come for Dad, and when he left, Jonathan followed him into the hallway. I think my brother understood that for me, this wasn't just the end of Dad's disease journey, it was the end of my caregiving journey as well.

I rested my head on Dad's chest to make sure his heart was at rest. I knew I wouldn't hear anything, and I didn't. I remained that way and wept at the departure of the man I'd taken care of in one way or another since Mom's passing.

After several minutes, I hugged him one last time, patted down his hair, and gently kissed him on the cheek good-bye.

FORTY-THREE

Five days later I stood in front of family, friends, and acquaintances who filled every church pew to honor Dad at his memorial service.

"November 23rd was my father's Independence Day. Almost three years ago, he was given a diagnosis that launched him, and the family, into the as-yet-unknown world of living with a terminal illness. You may be thinking, 'But, I thought your dad had Alzheimer's, not a terminal illness.' The sad news is that there is no cure for Alzheimer's. There are marginally effective treatments for the disease, but it is always fatal.

"Think, if you will, of incidents in your past that changed your life irreparably."

Those seated in the pews looked up at me. "No, I mean it, I would like you to take a few minutes."

I looked at those gathered at St. Benedicts Catholic Church in Wallingford and waited for them to answer my challenge. I sat down, thus giving them permission to think about my query without the threat of me breaking into their meditation before they were ready.

My support group friends were there, most without their loved ones. My best buddy, Pilar, and her boyfriend sat in the front pew with the rest of my family. Dad's Korean War buddies filled half a pew—each man rested his respective uniform hat in their lap. The balance of that pew was filled with three wait-staff employees from Blue Star Café. Both the soldiers and the restaurant employees greeted me prior to the service to tell me how much they missed Dad at their weekly gatherings. It felt special that they would honor my dad in this manner.

Three rows back, Virgilio sat with two Gazebo nursing assistants, as well as Polly Mitchell, the Seattle Gardens marketing person who treated Dad with such compassion and respect. The neighbors who lived on either side of our Wallingford house, as well as those who lived in the two houses directly across the street from the house, also took time off from their day to honor Dad and my family. Those same neighbors indicated that several other people from the neighborhood were at the church as well. Dennis and I hadn't yet made the rounds to introduce ourselves to everyone on our street, so this would be the first time we'd make their acquaintance. I think the remainder of those in attendance today were regular church members; even though it had been awhile since I'd attended Mass, I recognized a few of them.

When I saw that most of the attendees' heads were raised, I returned to the podium. "I guess you don't live as long as many of us have lived without having at least a half dozen such life-changing moments. Two out of three such moments that immediately came to my mind were devastating in their own ways, but in time, I climbed out of them and again started to experience the joys in life that continued to come my way unchecked.

"That was not the case when my father received an Alzheimer's diagnosis and his brain started to betray him. We lost a wee bit of him—inch by inch, second by second—so that at the time of his death, the essence of who he was had become enmeshed in the plaques and tangles of his brain. That was not supposed to happen to my dad. You see, Alzheimer's is a disease that happens to other people. You know . . . the coworker a few cubicles away, a stranger behind you in the grocery line, a neighbor . . . not someone in your own family, right?

"Wrong. Dad, and us Quinn family members discovered that if Alzheimer's could happen to our family, it could happen to anyone's. How could someone with a life-lifting sense of humor who was also affectionate, giving, and intelligent, come down with one of the least humorous diseases known to man? Talk about being totally caught off guard—when we weren't paying attention Alzheimer's invaded a pretty darn awesome family, led by an extremely amazing father.

"In my eyes, Dad could do no wrong. Some of his jokes were a bit lame, but not for lack of trying." Several in the church laughed and nodded having no doubt been on the receiving end of the good jokes, and the bad.

"My dad was a very successful real estate broker which, if you know the industry, means a lot of time away from the family. But for some reason, I never felt neglected. I don't know if it was my mother who filled in the gaps or those gaps simply didn't exist, but somehow I never felt as though Dad wasn't available to me and my two siblings.

"Our dad was fair. He was strict without breaking our spirit. If ever I felt regret over my actions, it came about as a result of wishing I had done better because I knew better, and I knew better because I was taught better.

"Dad was a great example of how to enjoy life from a down-to-earth perspective, a perspective that did not require grandiose plans costing piles of money. The family took joy in many mundane experiences and found humor in most of them. Family picnic rained out? Have no fear, that meant the picnic would take place inside. Truth be told, some of my most memorable picnics were inside the house without the bugs that oftentimes abbreviated such adventures. When we picnicked indoors, us kids crawled under sheets that Dad had draped across the furniture to block out the household scenery to assist in carrying out the illusion of being outside.

"Dad was a master of practical jokes and managed to pull a doozy over on my sister and me on April 1st of our freshman and sophomore years in high school. When it was time to get up for school that day, Dad knocked on our door, peeked his head in and said, 'Rise and shine and give God the glory!' Let me tell you, we didn't feel like giving anyone the glory that morning. Dad made it worse by telling us that the local public high school—we went to the Catholic one you see—had April 1st off from school, and wasn't it crazy to have a day off for April Fool's Day? My sister and I were infuriated that such a lame holiday warranted a day off from school. Dad sympathized with our plight. 'Isn't it just like a non-religious school to observe such a heathen holiday like April Fool's Day?' This time we crawled out of bed and just as we stood at our bedsides feeling as though the world had surely dealt a bad hand to us observant Catholics, Dad said, 'Gotcha!'

"We weren't angry at the local public school anymore, we were mad at being sucked into that travesty of a wakeup call. I can still hear Dad laughing all the way down the hallway and into the kitchen to prepare breakfast. Why he never played that joke on Jonathan, I'll never know, but I guess he figured his son would never have fallen for such foolishness.

"As much as he excelled in his sense of humor, Dad also shined in the category of compassion and care. Mom opted to turn this responsibility over to Dad when either of us kids needed a boost of encouragement. Mom was capable of providing that boost, but Dad was better at it. When Patty struggled in the development of her drawing and painting skills, Dad offered to enroll her in the Seattle Academy of Arts so she could gain the confidence she needed to pursue her craft. My sister is still committed to her artistic pursuits and has exhibited many of her paintings at art galleries in Northern California where she resides."

I looked at my notes and started to chuckle. "This next story might surprise my sister-in-law, and embarrass Jonathan, but I'll tell it anyway. My brother wasn't always the ladies' man. Back in his high school days he lacked the confidence required to invite a girl to a dance, even a girl with whom he had been friends for quite some time." I saw Patty elbow Jonathan who had a smile on his face because he knew where this story was going.

"My brother wanted to call Rebecca but didn't know what he could possibly say that would make her agree to attend the dance with him. Dad sat down with Jonathan and wrote out a telephone script that my brother practiced over and over again—a script that managed to secure him a date with the girl of his dreams.

"Now, Jonathan wasn't driving yet so on the night of the dance, Dad drove my brother to Rebecca's house to pick her up. After Jonathan collected his date at the doorstep, he proudly walked back to the car, opened the back door for her, helped her into the back seat, and promptly shut the door on her and climbed into the front with Dad. That's when Dad said, 'Son, don't you think you might be more comfortable in the back with your date? Why don't you join her and then we'll be on our way.' What makes this episode so endearing, is that Dad didn't make fun of Jonathan, and never made him feel like the doofus my brother knew he was. Dad built us up, he never tore us down.

"He exhibited extraordinary care and support to me after my husband's fatal car accident. He was upset by the thoughtlessness and carelessness of the person who drank too much, got in his car, and wiped out the life of a very precious person. Dad showed his support in many ways, and one of those ways was to boycott alcohol. He never had a drinking problem, but he chose to abstain from the stuff from that point forward. Dad was a man of principle—in that incident and in many others throughout his life.

"These previous statements about my dad are all the more reason why Alzheimer's disease pisses me off." I turned toward the priest sitting to my right. "Sorry, Father Bill, but it really does." Father Bill just nodded and said, "It's okay."

I continued. "If it's true that cancer is no respecter of persons, it is equally true that Alzheimer's disease exhibits the same lack of respect. This disease is a murderer and I'm troubled by the millions of crimes it has gotten away with it.

"Alzheimer's is also a robber, not only because it robs a person of his or her memories and future, but also because it exacts an emotional price that few can afford. To be sure, monetary costs are a challenging force to be reckoned with, but many family caregivers and their loved ones would no doubt conclude that the emotional toll on a person far surpasses even the costliest of care fees paid.

"Until the person with Alzheimer's or other dementia becomes blissfully unaware of the disease that is murdering him, he has a front row seat to all that's happening. My dad was the first to know when his senior moments became more than a quirk of the aging process. It grieves me to imagine what he went through when he was alone with his thoughts, witnessing first hand where those thoughts were taking him." I paused and looked down at the podium. I needed to compose myself for fear of letting loose with either an award winning crying bout or an invective that would send everyone scurrying.

When I looked up again, I saw my brother making his way to where I stood. When he got there he put his arm around my shoulder, squeezed it, and whispered, "I'm here for you, say what you need to say."

I turned my notes face down on the stand and finalized my tribute, off the cuff. "Being a caregiver, or being the one cared for, is an inevitability all of us will face. Whether Alzheimer's, cancer, or any of the countless other debilitating illnesses that come knocking on the door of your once-secure home, you'll wear one of two roles:

caregiver or cared for. There's no way around it, and because there is no escape hatch, you will need all the help you can muster. I learned the hard way that caregiving is a team sport. Not all that long ago, my brother Jonathan here, helped me put the caregiving journey into sports terms. Let's see if I remember the gist of it . . ."

I turned to Jonathan for help and then I remembered. "Oh yeah . . . um, what's a pitcher without a catcher? A quarterback without a receiver? A point guard without a center? They're individuals, not a team."

Jonathan nodded in agreement.

"Caregiving should never be an individual effort because quite frankly, one person can't do it all. I learned that the hard way, at first living under the delusion that I could and should do it all, and ultimately discovering that I couldn't and shouldn't.

"I also learned that family should always be a priority. I discovered that to be true in my own situation, and I've observed the same in the lives of others with whom I've become acquainted throughout Dad's disease journey. When everything is falling apart around you, family will get you through *if you let them*. That was definitely the case for me."

I leaned into Jonathan and looked out over the faces of those I knew well, and those I didn't know at all, and decided that my time at the podium should come to an end.

"I started today's eulogy by talking about my father's Independence Day. On that day, Dad was liberated from the cognitive chains that stifled his genuine and loving essence, and that dramatically shut down his stately and classic Irish self. Another thing happened on that day—I was no longer Dad's caregiver, but in my case, I didn't feel liberated at all. I would have given anything for just one more day of frustrating abnormal normalcy with my dad, instead of losing him forever.

"But that was not to be. All journeys come to an end and none of us would rob our dying loved ones of their final escape to a destination towards which their lives had been headed ever since their own personal diagnosis day. Instead, I celebrate the man I was proud to call my father, and I celebrate that the devastating disease of Alzheimer's is finished robbing him, and the rest of the family, of a well-deserved enjoyable and healthy life.

"Here's a send-off that was contained in a toast my father said at my husband Dennis's and my wedding a little over a year ago: 'May the Lord welcome you in Heaven, at least an hour before the Devil knows you're dead.' I love you Dad."

Jonathan hugged me long and tight and then we both had a joint cry that was long overdue. Patty hustled to the front of the church and announced that a somewhat traditional post-memorial Irish wake would take place at the family house in Wallingford, and if anyone needed directions they could collect a map printout on the table at the back of the church.

• • • • •

As it turned out, the folks who attended the wake were limited to Dad's war friends, each member of my support group, a few of my neighbors, my best friend Pilar and her Adonis, Jack, and Father Bill. Patty and Gabe took charge of all things having to do with food and beverages. They put together a fine spread of corn beef and cabbage and a hefty pot of potato leek soup. The meal wouldn't be complete without the addition of three traditional Irish desserts: Chocolate Potato Cake, Bailey's Marble Cheesecake, and an Apple Amber. Patty made the main meal herself, but took advantage of Seattle's Irish Rose Bakery for the sweets. Man oh man, did we have a feast.

At the close of the evening, support members Frank and Eddie remained, as did my entire family, including Pilar and Jack. We shared some more Dad and Mom stories so each of us kids ended up being embarrassed by a tale or two. Dennis loved the opportunity to learn a bit more about us Quinns—especially when it meant hearing the secret Colleen stories I had yet to tell him—and he relished yet another chance to provide me with the same unconditional support on which I had relied the best part of two years.

FORTY-FOUR

When Dennis and I moved into the Wallingford house, we inherited a family's lifetime of memories and started to create our own, not the least of which was the celebration of Dad's life the end of last November. Soon after moving into the house, we added another dog to the household, a lazy bloodhound named Critter, which Ramona adored in her own doggie way. She tried in vain to get him to show some energy—any energy at all—but that was not to be with that ol' rescue hound.

A few weeks after Dad's death, Jonathan and Melanie's son, Kirby, announced he planned to apply to medical school to become either a gerontologist or a neurologist so he could fill the void that exists for such specialties. My nephew will break the short line of Quinn real estate brokers that Dad and Jonathan created, but he'll make a huge impact on the future of the world of the elderly. If Dad were still here he'd say, "Getting old sure beats the alternative." I certainly hope he's right, and I hope all of us will live to see the day when Alzheimer's is curable and preventable.

Six months after Dad's death, I still yearn for the comradery found at the caregiver support group so I keep up my monthly attendance. Even though my caregiver journey has ended, those of my other caregiver friends has not. I feel invested in their lives, just as they were in mine.

Almost monthly, the group receives new members and a few drop-ins. A couple months ago, Susie, a single mother, attended one of our support group meetings by using sick leave time from work. This caregiver had already spent three years trying to juggle her job and her family with her mother's early-onset dementia. Because her mother couldn't be left alone, Susie scrambled week after week to find trustworthy people to stay at the house while she worked through her 7 am to 4 pm shift as an Information Technology employee.

Susie made a decent wage, but that amount fell into the not-so-great category when her mother's care needs increased faster than they could be addressed. Her mother needed more than just the friendly church-sponsored chore ministry on which Susie had previously relied. She went through a local staffing agency to hire a Certified Nursing Assistant to care for her mother five days a week from 6:30 am to 3:30 pm to augment one and a half hours of church sponsored companion care from 3:30 to 5 pm. Each day, Susie rushed home at the end of her shift to relieve the church companion, hoping her mom hadn't required any professional assistance between the time when the nursing assistant left and the church lady took over.

Once home Susie prepared dinner for the household which included two junior high-aged children. She then monitored their homework assignments and parceled out as much attention as her two pre-teens demanded. That still left Susie to help her mother with her end-of-day tasks, after which Susie had "free" time until the CNA arrived the following morning—free time that was often interrupted by her mother getting up in the middle of the night and wandering the house. Unfortunately, Susie attended just that one support meeting. As much as she could greatly benefit from what it had to offer, I was certain her attendance was not an option with all she had going on.

Several months back, Eddie found a relatively affordable housing situation for his wife, but that affordable memory care was located in the city of Auburn, thirty miles south of Seattle. He struggled greatly with the decision to move Katherine out of their house, even attempting in-home care, but his wife's unpredictable, and sometimes violent, behavior ended that prospect just two weeks after it started. Katherine slapped the caregiver one day, and when a different caregiver arrived the next day, Eddie couldn't leave for work because his wife screamed and stormed through the house slamming doors. Eddie cancelled the caregiver service and got busy touring facilities.

Their son, Richard, stayed with his mom while Eddie and Frank made the rounds, not having the luxury of considering facilities close to his home. As Eddie put it, the conveniently located facilities charged rates that were way out of his network. The affordable care he found amounted to $3200 per month, an amount he's certain will drain the coffers before too long. But they didn't qualify for Medicaid so that's the hand they were dealt—private pay all the way.

Mary still attends the meetings, even after her husband William's passing. Her friendship connection with Victoria continues, with Mary now more able to provide the emotional support Victoria needs as George progresses towards end-stage Alzheimer's. Now and then, Mary accompanies Victoria to story time at George's memory care unit and even subs for Victoria when she doesn't feel up to it.

Kelly retired from her job as an attorney to be more available to her partner, Donna. They went on a cruise to Alaska—something Donna had always wanted to do—and Kelly spent part of her pension fund to upgrade to a larger cruise cabin that would accommodate Donna's wheelchair. The physical symptoms of Donna's Parkinson's seem to be progressing faster than the dementia aspect of the disease. Both women are painfully aware of what awaits them in the months ahead.

Rose's sister Sophia continues to decline, so much so that the doctors feel she may have less than three months to live. The muscle atrophy and resultant inactivity have taken their toll on her vital organs—she already experienced one bout of pneumonia from which she almost didn't recover. But Sophia continues to enjoy Billy Joel's singing and is rarely seen without earbuds which have become the most important accessory she owns.

Frank's son Sean shadows my husband at the Veterans Hospital in his effort to be an additional support to those service people recovering from physical and psychological wounds. Sean still has struggles with which to contend—not the least of which is ongoing reduced cognitive function—but he figures it's more constructive to be as active as possible now than to focus on how that may change later. Dennis enjoys his time with Sean. My husband considers Sean to be the little brother he never had growing up.

I enrolled in training to become an Alzheimer's caregiver support group facilitator but the closer the class date approached, the more I realized I wasn't ready. The Alzheimer's Association volunteer coordinator put my name on the first training of next year. By then I'm certain the emotional wounds of caring for and losing Dad will have sufficiently healed to try my hand at it again.

· · · · ·

Last night, Dennis and I returned home from a visit to Whidbey Island to celebrate Pilar and Jack's wedding. I'm thrilled to be adding another member to the family with Jack Pritchard. Dennis and Jack get along great, so we make a point of getting together with Pilar and him every month. And of course both Pilar and I have personal guest rooms at the offing so whether in Seattle or Whidbey, the accommodations are always covered.

Today, I'm continuing the new Calvary Cemetery ritual set in motion back in November of last year. After I drove up to Mom and Dad's section, I left Ramona and Critter in the back of the Subaru and made my way to the joint plot. The salmon-colored headstone bears the names of Constance Patricia Quinn: May 6, 1932 – October 13, 2007 and Patrick Craig Quinn: January 10, 1927 – November 23, 2014. I sat cross-legged on the grass and got warmed up for my visit.

"Hey, Mom and Dad, did you hear the one about the elderly gentleman who was invited to his friend's house for dinner one evening? The friend was impressed by the way his elderly buddy preceded every request to his wife with endearing terms: Honey, My Love, Darling, Sweetheart, Pumpkin, etc.

"The couple had been married almost 70 years and they were clearly still very much in love. When the wife was in the kitchen, the friend leaned over and said to his old buddy, 'I think it's wonderful that after all these years, you still call your wife those loving pet names.'

"The old man hung his head. 'To be truthful, I forgot her name about 10 years ago.'"

"Pretty good, huh? Here's another that's a real knee slapper: Last year Brittney replaced all the windows in her house with those expensive double pane energy efficient kind. Several months later, she received a call from the contractor complaining that his work had been completed a whole year and Brittney had yet to pay for them.

"Boy, oh, boy did they have an argument. Brittney said, 'Just because I'm blonde doesn't mean I'm stupid.' And then she proceeded to tell the contractor what the fast-talking sales guy had told her when he gave his spiel about the windows: 'within one year, the windows would pay for themselves.'"

"I know, pretty lame, that's why I thought you'd get a kick out of it. Wait, before I go, here's another you're sure to appreciate: Three men died and went to heaven . . ."

View other Black Rose Writing titles at www.blackrosewriting.com/books and
use promo code **PRINT** to receive a **20% discount** when purchasing.

BLACK🌑ROSE
writing™

CPSIA information can be obtained
at www.ICGtesting.com
Printed in the USA
FSOW01n1040150617
35223FS